GW00457080

# JOIN MY LEON M A EDWARDS CLUB

Leon M A Edwards Club members get free books, ahead of publications. So you can enjoy the book and form an opinion of how it made you feel.

Members only get emails about any promotions and when the next book is ready for receiving.

See the back of the book for details on how to sign up.

# JANE KNIGHT

## A SPY AMONG US

### LEON MA EDWARDS

*I would like to dedicate this book to Andrea, Alina and Lilia for leaving me to it, to write.*

*I would also like to dedicate this book to my dad who passed away on Monday 25th January 2021. He will be sorely missed by his five children, eight grandchildren and a loving wife.*

# ACKNOWLEDGMENTS

Thank God for giving me the confidence to start writing and the ability to write a story.

# 1

## STORY SO FAR

May 2020.

MY NAME IS Jane Knight and I am thirty-seven years old. I have a degree in Accountancy and before working for The Agency, I worked in a practice firm specialising in tax and forensic accounting.

I am four feet and ten inches tall, so I am seen as very short. I am an English Caucasian with natural bleached-blonde hair.

My friends from university have said in the past that I look like Erin Heatherton, as I have a slim face and nose with light visible freckles on my cheeks, chin and forehead. I have an hourglass figure, so I have a slim waist with hips and a flat stomach. I do not wear makeup as I have never had the opportunity to properly learn how to wear it well. I made myself look like a clown one time. My voice is soft with no accent, due to living in Buckinghamshire.

My choice of clothing is a pair of slim bootcut jeans with Skechers. I either wear a polo shirt with no label or a slim-fit woollen pullover. I keep my hair in a ponytail the majority of the time.

I HAVE WORKED for an established division within the Military Intelligence Six building since the middle of 2015. I have been a field agent since late 2016.

It is a stand-alone department called 'The Agency'. I was recruited purely by chance when I was invited to go to my friend Anthea's engagement party. I was one of only two single people there among thirty plus guests. As a result, everyone sat next to their respective partners, and that naturally left me and one other single person to sit next to each other.

Because I am shy, when he made the effort to spark a conversation, I could imagine it was like pulling teeth. After several attempts to get my attention, we talked about our occupations and interests. A few weeks later, I was asked to join a recently created agency.


THERE ARE ONLY twenty of us who work in the agency, but we are gradually expanding after our first few successful assignments. Because we are a small division, we were given floor space by Military Intelligence Six to work in. We still do not have the budget to afford our own building and it will be a long while before that happens.

The office was given a new dark grey carpet. We were also given new cubical light grey desks. The desks are laid out in five columns by three rows. My desk is in one of the end columns. Our floor manager has his own office at the end, which has glass walls. I assume it is so he can oversee the floor from his desk.


THE AGENCY SPECIALISES in gathering intelligence on companies that fund terrorism. The companies are based both in the United Kingdom and abroad. We investigate companies around the world that have an office registered in the United Kingdom.

These are companies that may be supplying their resources such as factories, machinery and plant to persons or groups involved in terrorism. It can also include component stock or finished product stock and cash.

The end users are persons or groups that are a threat to the United Kingdom. The end users are not necessarily British or immigrants. They can be any nationality from around the world.

Our floor manager has, over the past twelve months, built up communication with key intelligence services in America, France, Germany, China, Spain, the Cayman Islands and Switzerland. This is to allow a free flow of information within the intelligence community.


THE DEPARTMENT HAS TWENTY STAFF, including myself, and two from Military Intelligence Five.

The twenty staff are broken down into seven field agents, five information technology staff, five analysts and three reviewers. Charles and I are two of the seven field agents.

.   .   .

THE SEVEN FIELD agents travel domestically and internationally, gathering intelligence information such as details of component stock, chemical stock, delivery notes, goods received notes and internal management accounts. The field agents are given information on what to look for. The names of chemicals and materials that go into bombs are supplied to the field agents. This is so that they know what intelligence to collect.

THE TEAM of five information technologists helps to run the mainframe, server and internal internet. They also look after the storage of written reports, emails and evidence. They supply and support hardware such as desktops, printers, laptops and hard drives. They also provide key cards to allow our field agents to override security doors. They are also creating software to allow a universal serial hub to automatically extract data. The department also helps to keep track of where their six agents are.

THE FIVE ANALYSTS collate the information supplied by the field agents. The intelligence collected is then recorded in a report that they write, using an internal template that they can fill in using their own style of writing. The report cannot be suggestive and factual, but should not include personal opinions. They also use the companies' financial reports. They retrieve those from Companies House and the companies' websites.

The financial reports are used to ascertain who the officers of the company are and what industry it is trading in. The officers are the chief executive officer, the vice presidents, directors and chief finance officer.

The analysts also investigate the background of each officer in terms of business associates, friends and interests.

The report can be ten pages long with about five thousand words.

THE THREE REVIEWERS proofread our reports. Not to check our grammar but to see that we have provided an impartial recommendation.

THE DEPARTMENT WAS CREATED because MI6, MI5, Government Communications Headquarters and the police were all stretched already. The current entities are already struggling to deal with direct terrorism. There was a gap in monitoring indirect terrorist threats and actually targeting the beginning of the supply chain rather than the end. So, the new agency I work for solely targets the indirect terror threats which means targeting the companies.

. . .

I HAVE MADE some really good friends since working here, including a guy by the name of Barney Cooper who looks after I.T for the department.

Barney has similar features to Jonah Hill, the actor who played a geek in 'Super Bad'. Barney has the same hairstyle with the same thick curly hair like an afro and unshaven with a scraggy beard; a poor attempt. He is six feet tall. He is originally from Scotland and has a thick Scottish accent.

His style of dress is khaki trousers, a T-shirt and a zip-up hoody. He wears plimsolls for shoes.

IN BARNEY'S PERSONAL LIFE, he has a long-term girlfriend named Katherine, or Kate for short. He and his partner are happily in love and have a lot in common.

They met eight years ago when Barney first came to London from Southampton when he went to Oktoberfest in Covent Garden. She has lived in London for four years after leaving Wales to study archaeology in London. She then found a career in one of the museums in London as a curator.

He is originally from Glasgow and she is originally from Pumsaint, a village in Wales.

They share a rented flat in Brixton, not far from the London underground, behind the main roads.

I HAVE a work partner who recently became my first ever boyfriend. His name is Charles May. He is over six feet tall and reminds me of Idris Elba. He is black but his skin is light like some Jamaicans. He is clean-shaven and his hair is a crew cut, grade one. He walks with a swagger of "I don't give a damn". He is wearing a three-piece suit in dark blue with brown polished shoes. His voice is not rough but soft like a sophisticated Caucasian man. You would not want to meet him at night in a dark alley. His face is slim and almost chiselled. He has a flat stomach and I can only guess that he has the definition of a six-pack but not too obvious.

He taught me self defence and how to shoot a handgun and rifle. He was matter-of-fact and very professional when I was struggling on the training course. I was so bad that, in the end, he taught me where the pressure points are on a body and told me to focus on that.

OUR BOSS IS MILES STONES, who looks a bit like Benedict Cumberbatch but with black hair, side-parted to his left. He is clean-shaven and wears nice cologne that I can smell from a couple of feet away. He is someone I used to fancy when I first met him, but that was a long time ago now.

MILES' boss, who Charles and I now report to, as well as Miles, is Mary Johnson. She is Caucasian, in her early sixties with short black hair, down to her shoulder. Her face is pale and she wears red lipstick. She wears dark two-piece skirt suits. She has an authoritative appearance but has no sense of humour. She used to work for MI6 as well and was put in charge of the new agency.

OUR FIRST ASSIGNMENT was to gather enough intel to close down a company that allegedly supplied Novichok nerve agent, that killed the father and daughter in Salisbury. The person who owned the company was Vladimir Mashkov.

During the assignment, we found out that there was going to be a deal going down to supply arms to terrorists. We managed to prevent the exchange from going ahead. During the assignment, I also stumbled on an unknown group established by someone called Ivor Peteski. He told me that they are a society. Charles and I later found out that the unknown group is called 'The Order'.

We assumed that Vladimir died during the interruption of the firearms deal. The assignment gave us more questions than answers.

What is the society, if they are called that?

Why was Ivor at a meeting in the Cayman Islands with Vladimir, after informing on him to us?

What did Vladimir have on Ivor to persuade him not to leave the society?

Where is Vladimir's body?

Where did Natalia's body go?

What were the smart boxes doing in a warehouse full of weapons?

OUR SECOND ASSIGNMENT was tracking down an escapee that MI6 were involved in. We were asked to use our analysis skills to track her down, then have MI6 collect her. At the time we were tracking her down, we stumbled on her plans to seek revenge.

There were three rockets; one to take out an industrial plant, one for a man by the name of Jabulani Botha, and one to disrupt a meeting.

We could only stop two of the rockets. So, we allowed one of them to head to Jabulani Botha who killed Svana's parents.

We managed to prevent her from taking out the industrial plant and foiling the meeting.

SINCE OUR FIRST TWO ASSIGNMENTS, we have been on nineteen more missions, completing all twenty-one missions.

Charles and I have not heard any more about The Order since our second mission. Each of our other field trips has been as dangerous as the last. We have had some scary moments where cities and provinces were almost swiped out.

OUR CURRENT ASSIGNMENT takes us to China. We are staying at the 'Shenzhen Futian Wyndham Grand Hotel' in Shenzhen, in the province of Guangdong.

Our room is wide and open-plan, like a studio apartment but without the kitchen. It is very contemporary with neutral colours on the walls, bedding and furniture. Our room overlooks the city skyline.

WE HAVE BEEN in China for only a couple of days to arrange hiring a car to drive to a warehouse. During our two days here, we have explored the city and sampled the cuisine.

We have noticed that we occasionally receive strange stares when sight-seeing. Charles explains that, in China, the government are trying to discourage racism, but people choose not to adapt. He also knew that he would face some racial prejudice and was prepared for it.

I express disappointment and know that the world is not perfect when it comes to racial equality. I also know that I will be favoured more than him because of my skin. We have many discussions like this in private which sometimes makes it hard for me to swallow the bitter pill. Charles always makes excuses for people who judge his appearance. I know there is no excuse for it and that is one of the reasons why I love him so much.

I know that is the reason why we fit together because we both understand how we are affected by external entities. We comfort each other in our own unique ways.

WE ARE in our hotel in Shenzhen. It is after eight o'clock in the evening and we are going over tomorrow's visit. Our cover is designed completely around getting us inside the premises. Barney has given us identification that should get us in without any questions. Once we finish clearing our agenda, we both go in the shower to get ready to go out for dinner.

. . .

CHARLES WANTS to go for a meal and asks me to cut his hair before we go. He normally prepares his own hair.

I have only shaven his head once and he critiqued my work and we ended up having an argument. I wonder if he will judge my second attempt as harshly.

He is annoying, telling me how to cut his hair when I have not even begun yet. Charles tries to push my buttons by saying that he can cut my hair better than my hairdresser. I tell him to be quiet while I concentrate.

WHEN WE COME out of the shower, we put on the hotel's brilliant white bathrobes to finish getting ready. Charles has me shave his hair to grade zero as it has grown half an inch too long. I agree reluctantly, as I remember the last time when we had reservations about how well I trimmed his hair.

AFTER I HAVE FINISHED, he spends ages checking himself in the mirror trying to find any excuse to give me grief.

He thinks I have made a gouge in his grade zero hair. I playfully hit him in the arm and he pretends to be in pain. I go to walk away and sulk when he grabs me from behind. We both laugh and he kisses me on my cheek with his strong arms around me. I turn round to face him and we end up not making it out to dinner.

I TAKE his hand and walk him to the bed and push him backwards and watch him fall. I kneel between his legs and slide my hand inside his robe.

I keep eye contact with Charles as I begin to caress the end of his manhood. I use the tips of my fingers to tease him and eventually, the palm of my hand to stroke his full length.

Charles rests his head back and closes his eyes to intensify the feeling. I always enjoy making my partner aroused. I find his quirky groans comforting, like he is stirring in his sleep. I feel so turned on every time I watch him reacting to my touch. It never takes him long to get a full erection.

I crawl onto the bed and rest my body between his legs and make him squirm as I swirl my tongue and flick it over the end. Charles' body jerks occasionally, like a bolt of lightning has surged through him.

Occasionally, I laugh to myself as I enjoy seeing my long-term partner getting turned on.

As I continue to focus on his end, I slowly slide both my hands along his length, feeling his uneven surface.

CHARLES LOVES the way Jane uses her tongue and the feel of the surface stimulating the end of his manhood. He finds closing his eyes intensifies the experience. He cannot control the way his body has a life of its own as it twitches from Jane's touch.

He can feel himself beginning to ejaculate as Jane builds up momentum, carrying him along like a small boat in a raging storm.

He cannot help breaking out a knee-jerking groan. His body stiffens like an electric current is rushing through it.

WITHOUT WARNING, I get startled when I feel a splash on my face that almost goes into my eyes. Charles cannot stop flowing out like a burst main pipe.

I know that it is a build-up because of us having no intimacy for a long time due to work commitments and the long hours.

We both miss this and, if we had a choice, we would never leave the bedroom. We would hide ourselves away from the world.

Sometimes, I wish we were in another career that allowed time for us, instead of saving the country from potential threats.

2

# TWENTY-SECOND MISSION

The next morning, we wake up not wanting to leave the bed. We lie there for a while and decide to order breakfast in our room.

After breakfast, we pack our belongings and prepare our story for when we arrive at the warehouse. Our plan is to appear as external auditors for the company, who have been asked to count the inventory inside the warehouse. If we are asked any questions, we tell them that it was an impromptu request.

To dress as the part of two auditors, Charles wears a three-piece suit with a corporate tie and I wear a two-piece trouser suit with a blouse. It is agreed that I take the lead because I have an accountancy background.

Our luggage is left in the storage room at reception. We use the car we hired when we first arrived.


WE ARE NOT suspicious of the company funding any radicals, but the government are considering using the Chinese telecommunication company's services.

The Chinese company are to supply the country's telecom masts to improve mobile data usage and coverage. The government feels that the nation is behind compared to other countries.

Rumours began circulating that the company's technology could extract data from

Our government is worried that the company will use its technology to steal sensitive information and use it against us. They want The Agency to use our skills to find out if they could be a threat. Our boss, Miles, sends us out to investigate.

One of our analysts wrote a report on a company that manufactures components for mobile telecom masts. They found that there could be a risk of transferring personal information back to their offices in China.

Charles and I have to gather evidence that can confirm whether the company have designed a product to steal people's personal data.

Barney has hacked into the company's server to find out where they keep their technology inventory and designs. He sent the co-ordinates to our mobiles.

WHILE WE HAVE BEEN STAYING in Shenzhen, we have been enjoying Chinese cuisine and culture. For breakfast, we had a choice of 'Soybean milk and deep-fried dough stick', 'Steamed sweet bun with custard-filled inside' or 'Pancakes with egg'. The hotel has western breakfast items, such as toast, cereal and boiled eggs, but it is their version, so they seem like they are making an attempt.

For lunch, we focused on noodle dishes seasoned and garnished with seasoning and sauce. Dinner consisted of rice, various meats and a side of steamed vegetables.

We notice that the culture is a mixture of local traditional Chinese roots and aspects of American fashion and appearance.

Charles has noticed that the small independent businesses tend to find it strange seeing a black person. I had to have Charles bring it to my attention. But the branded chains, like the hotel we are staying at, are multicultural and are not fazed by other foreign visitors.

After experiencing a couple of strange glares, we decided to avoid local business premises.

DURING OUR DRIVE THERE, I remember being surprised on our first day here that I never knew the Chinese drive on the same side of the road as England. However, they do not have roundabouts.

To get us around Shenzhen, we use the built-in sat-nav and have the instructions in English.

We drive for thirty minutes to arrive at the destination where we will carry out our assignment.

WE ARRIVE at a remote building owned by a Chinese telecommunication company. The site houses the company's archives of purchase orders, goods received notes, purchase invoices and an inventory of computer components. Based on information gathered by our intelligence sources, we know that the storage facility is at a remote site that is guarded by a skeleton crew of ten security guards.

We are travelling outside Shenzhen, towards the Deep Bay, heading West. The road is turning from tarmac to dirt road as we reach the outskirts of the city, twenty miles out. We are aiming to get there for three o'clock.

Our cover story is that we have been seconded from London to Shenzhen for a year. We have been asked to audit a storage facility. We are going in as the company's external auditors.

My background, before joining The Agency, was in accountancy and so it is perfect for this type of job. My partner, who is also my boyfriend, was transferred from MI6 to our agency, an extended branch of MI6, which takes on companies that fund terrorism or are an apparent threat to the UK. We take on work that other intelligence communities do not want to get involved in. We are seen as the underdogs, dealing with the menial work that no one else likes doing.

We are on our twenty-second assignment since The Agency was set up in 2015. We are to collect paperwork relating to the Chinese company supplying 5G to the UK. The government want to know if their components in the telecommunication masts can transmit sensitive data, outside the public eye, back to China. They asked our agency to gather the information as we are skilled in espionage. We are to find either blueprints or diagrams of the technology.

We arrive at the location and can see the building from outside the grounds. It appears more of a compound than a storage facility as it is concrete rather than bricks and mortar, or corrugated steel.

We approach the security entrance with the cabin and guard on my partner's side.

After a few seconds of showing our fake employment cards from the audit firm, we are allowed through. The security guard is wearing a black army officer's suit and appears to be in his late thirties with thick straight black hair.

He points to the building in front of us and tells us to go in there and also says that there are parking bays outside.

We realise that the site is military, which makes sense as the Chief Executive Officer was in the army. He must still have connections with the military to be allowed to use their property. I see another building, opposite the one that we will be going into, that is a single-storey construction. There are five army trucks with green canvas covers on the back. I notice that there is a helicopter beyond the building we are going into. I do not know what type it is but I have seen that type before.

My partner boasts that he would be able to fly that, now he has gained his pilot licence through employment.

When we step out of the Land Rover that we hired, I look past the compound perimeter and notice that there are miles of green fields.


THE CONCRETE BUILDING has a hexagonal shape. Inside the building is also hexagonal, with half the building having upper floors. The other side has no floors and you can see right to the ceiling above. The only way to get to each floor is via a cage lift.

We can see that there are three floors above us. The ground floor is bare and empty. We take the lift to the first floor.

There are long rows of 'Roller Racking' systems from floor to ceiling. Each roller racking system has multiple compartments on shelves. To get to the shelves, you have to spin a three-pronged wheel to slide the tall shelves along either side.


WE HAVE ALREADY SPENT over an hour checking the ground floor, first and second floor. I wonder if we have been given the right location.

We are halfway through checking each racking system and we are slowly losing the will to live.

Charles gets my attention as he whispers aloud, 'Hey, I think I've found what we are looking for.'

I am a couple of yards away and so run over and broach his personal space; 'Let me see. Yes, you're right. Take photos of the diagrams on your mobile and send them to Barney. That's enough. And take the original. No components here?'

Charles thinks I am being bossy, 'Yes, Jane. Anything else?'

I respond cheekily, 'Yes. A kiss.'


CHARLES MOVES me so that I have my back against the shelf. He wants to rekindle last night as he kisses me passionately and forget why we are here. I feel like we are in a library and we shouldn't be canoodling. We end up lying on the floor with him hovering over me, on his elbows. We continue being intimate with no rush to leave. Even though we have been together for more than three years, I never tire of doing this.


THE SECURITY GUARD manning the gate has his usual call from his manager to find if there have been any unusual activities. He says that it is the same as any other day. In the same breath, he remembers the two people who came in.

He tells his manager that two auditors came to check the inventory. The manager is puzzled as every visitor is passed through him. This is so that he can let the security guard know he is okay to show them through. The guard knows this, but because they said they were auditors, he did not think any more of it.

His manager has no knowledge of a last-minute inventory check. He is suspicious and puts the guard on hold. His manager keeps him on hold and goes away to check with the accounts department.

After a few minutes, he returns to the guard and tells him that there is no appointment for an unscheduled audit. He tells the guard to raise the alarm and have them detained.

The security guard smacks his hand on the red button located on the wall of the cabinet. A few seconds later, a siren blares out with a deafening wailing sound. Nine other security guards come running from the building opposite the archive station, securing the inner boundary of the storage building.


WHILE CHARLES and I make out like two teenagers, we unexpectedly hear the alarm going and wonder why. We then hear the lift starting as it makes an unmistakable whirring noise. We jump to our feet and stare at each other, disappointed at our interruption. We wait first to see who comes out of the lift, as we peer between files to see the lift door.

When the door slides open, men in army uniform coming running out and start searching for us.


AS WE QUIETLY RUN IN the opposite direction to find a place to hide, we are noticed and they begin firing their sub-machine guns. We crouch to avoid being hit. Charles gets his handgun out in readiness as we sit behind one of the roller racking systems.

During the chaos, my phone rings and I instinctively answer with a quizzical voice, 'Hello?'

It is my accountant. 'Have I caught you at a bad time?'

I notice Charles is annoyed with me. 'Just going through some paperwork.'

My accountant seems distracted; 'What is that noise in the background?'

I think on my feet; 'It's fireworks. What is the reason for the call?'

My accountant wants to warn me, 'You seem to have made a substantial amount of money. You have ten...'

Bullets are whizzing over our heads and making it hard to hear what he is saying. They are tearing through the racks like they are made of paper. The files are getting ripped to pieces and floating in the air.

I think about the guards catching up with us and abruptly continue the conversation; 'I put the money in a high-interest account. That would explain the ten grand interest.'

Charles eventually begins firing back and the sound of his gun is blocking my hearing.

My accountant appears to disagree. 'I'm talking more like...'

I close my free ear with my finger as I try to hear him clearer, but there is no improvement.

I can see Charles wants me to hang up, so I say, 'Really sorry. Have to go. Call me later.'

Once I hang up, Charles pulls me to follow him towards signs for the roof. There are some metal girder stairs that we run up.

Sparks are flying off the railings and staircase as we run up to the roof.


THE STAIRS LEAD to the dark grey concrete ceiling and we see a black metal rectangular hatch door. We go through the door and then bolt it from the outside. We then look around the edge of the roof for a ladder against the building, or even a rope. I get spooked when I go to one side and there is a sheer drop to the sea. We must be a hundred feet above sea level. We do not find anything to help our escape. I check to see if the hatch is being prised open with force but there is no sign.

Out of nowhere, we hear machine guns outside and sparks fly off the edge of the roof at the front of the building. We stay in the centre and drop to the floor.

Charles sees something above and says, 'Time to buckle up.'

I see what he is on about and say, 'Let's do it.'

Charles notices a black wire above us which must be a telephone cable. We take our belts from around our waists and prepare to slide to the ground with them.

He goes first and I follow behind him, leaving a few seconds so we do not collide with one another. While we glide along the cable, more bullets whizz past our ears as they try to kill us. When we are close to the ground, we let ourselves drop and then roll along the tarmac.

When we get out bearings, we see our ride and run towards the hire car.

ONE OF THE guards sees the two fake auditors running towards their car. He remembers that there are weapons in the back of the five military trucks. He quickly runs over to one of them and breaks open one of the crates. He sees that is has a PF-98 rocket launcher. He takes it out and searches for a missile in the other crates.

He breaks open a couple more until he finds one and shoves it inside the barrel of the launcher. He then gets into a firing position and aims at the car.

WE ARE STILL BEING FIRED upon as sparks fly near our feet and we use our arms for cover. We are a stone's throw away when I hear a whizzing noise and then a flash behind the car. Then there is a huge explosion that throws us backwards onto the ground.

I cannot believe they fired a rocket at our car! 'That was overkill.'

Charles agrees, 'They only had to shoot the tyres.'

I wonder what we will do next. 'Great. How do we get out of this mess?'

Charles is thinking something else; 'I loved that car. I have another way out.'

Charles grabs my arm so that I will follow behind him. We run in the opposite direction, away from the guards. I notice he is taking us towards the helicopter. We are still being fired at and hide behind the storage building. When we think we have an opportunity, we quickly make a dash for the helicopter. I see the bullets bounce off the skin of the gunship, leaving black scorch marks.

We go to either side and pull up the glass doors to climb inside and quickly shut them back down.

We are safe now and ignore the pinging noise of bullets smacking against the glass and metal. Charles presses buttons on the control panel of the cockpit above us and in between us. I hear the engine beginning to warm up with a whirring noise. The rotor slowly spins when it builds up momentum. While we wait to be able to take off, we see another launcher aiming at us. Charles tries to work out how to operate the weapons of the Apache. He sees a red flip-up pad and pushes it up to see a flat triangular button. I ask him what it is for and he says he assumes it is for the missiles. We stare at each other and wonder if it will work. I glance to my right to see the missiles attached to the side. The man is ready to fire another rocket at us.

Charles quickly pushes the button and a huge whistling noise follows behind a missile that sounds like a firework being set off. With great speed, it impacts with one of the military trucks behind the man with the PF-98. All five trucks instantly burst into a ball of flames, followed by a deafening sound.

We see a military truck driving into the compound which we assume the guy at the gate ordered. Charles wastes no time turning the helicopter to face the additional threat. Without hesitation, he fires another missile and, in seconds, incinerates the truck.

We check if there are any new threats but no one is in sight to worry about. Charles finally takes off and takes his time turning the helicopter to face the sea. We then casually fly away without any urgency.

Charles has worked up an appetite and suggests, 'I noticed a nice restaurant when we first came here. There is plenty of room for parking. Do you like sweet and sour chicken?'

I cannot believe he can think of food after narrowly escaping, but I answer, 'I prefer crispy duck.'

We both smile at each other and head for the restaurant.

# 3

## BACK ON SCHEDULE

There is a meeting in Spain at a secluded multi-million-euro Tuscan-style mansion in the south. The property is wide, stretching the length of three football fields and half the width of a football field. The middle section is the tallest section with a lift inside and three floors. The four sections on either side descend like stairs.

THE HOUSE IS OWNED by a man called Xavier Hark who is in his late sixties now. He has some grey hair mixed in with his original black ones. He is bald on top with grade two hair on the sides and back. He has a full black beard. He is six foot tall and slim. He wears a two-piece suit and a white shirt. His ties are corporate, with diagonal stripes.

XAVIER HEADS A SOCIETY CALLED 'THE ORDER', as in a new order that was established in 1940 by his father. His father had just turned thirty when he had the idea of making a perfect world. His father died in his eighties in 1995.

Xavier's family is from old money back in the late 1800s. His great-great-grandfather became an industrialist. His father's old money was not enough for him. His father had an idea of a perfect world without war by creating one single country.

His family knew they could not do it alone and so he sought out like-minded people within their business circle. He found twenty-one similar wealthy families who liked the idea. They decided to give themselves the nickname 'The Order' as in the new order.

They then wanted to find someone to make it happen. Their first patsy was Adolf Hitler. Since then, they have tried to use other means. There were ten attempts, the first in 1956 and the last in 1995.

When Xavier's father passed away, he was then put in charge of running the organisation. He has been making his father's legacy become a reality since his father passed away.

XAVIER HAS, for the first time, arranged for the twenty-one men and women, who represent their families, to come to his house.

He has arranged for them to come over so they can finalise their plans for coming even closer to reaching their goal. The meeting is taking place in the evening under the cover of darkness. He is holding the conference in his large dining room.

They have flown in, and driven, from around the world as they migrated from Germany and changed their names to suit the country, over three generations ago. The people who arrived in cars own Mercedes, Rolls Royce, Bentley and Ferrari vehicles. The people who flew in travelled by their own private jets. They are already sat around his solid mahogany circular table with bottles of red, white and rosé wine.

The men are wearing tailored suits, a mixture of single and double-breasted and in a variety of colours They are in their forties and fifties.

The women are in dress suits of similar colours and they are of similar ages.

Xavier is ready to take the meeting, 'I have called you here because we are finally in reach of our agenda. Vladimir's company has mass-supplied the smart boxes around the world. We have achieved Brexit to destabilise Europe and finally have the funds to rebuild. We were only delayed by three years due to our fallen member, Svana Chase. We can confirm that 80% of the world have our product.'

Another member has a question; 'What about Jane Knight and Charles May? They are still causing mayhem closing down some of our operations.'

Xavier gently smiles in his chair. 'When we complete our task, they will be held to us if they are still alive. We will complete in the first week of September.'

A second member speaks out; 'We have an issue. The software to carry out the task has a few teething problems. While rigorously testing the system for robustness, we noticed a problem. Our current programmer cannot resolve the problem.'

Xavier is not worried and assures them, 'I will have that resolved. One of our people has made contact about another potential problem. I was originally going to have them killed. Instead, we can use them to resolve the glitch. We will still be on schedule.'

A third member appears impatient, demanding, 'How long will it take for the problem to be resolved?'

Xavier waves his arms to calm him down, 'We are looking at a month to rewrite the section of code. The machine is already in place. We are really close to the finish line.'

A fourth member has a question; 'Where will we congregate?'

Xavier can feel everyone is feeling tense now that they are so close. 'I will inform you a few weeks before we engage.'

The meeting lasts for thirty minutes, and afterwards, they have dinner and then retire to another room where they are given a nightcap.

During this time, Xavier walks over to a man by the name of Ivor Peteski.

Ivor was put in charge of his family business when his father passed away almost four years ago. He delved into his family business when dealing with his father's will and estate. He quickly understood that The Order existed but did not know the official name. He saw it as a secret society and was not sure why it began.

He used to work for a commercial bank in London and did not know that his employer had this society as their clients. He investigated the accounts and realised that their transactions were held in unnamed accounts.

Around the time when The Agency was created, Miles was approached by him to look into it. Miles had already created a contact through him on completely separate matters and thought he could help with finding companies using his bank that fund terrorism.

Miles sent Jane to meet up with Ivor to gather intel on their first suspected company.

Ivor is Caucasian in his late thirties. His hair is thick, wavy and black with flecks of grey. He keeps his hair floppy and brushed back with light gel.

His face is square, slim and clean-shaven and he has aged well.

He is six foot six tall with long legs and a long body frame. He is slim and athletic. He has a similar appearance to Colin Firth. His accent is English and posh as he was educated in London.

His personality is conservative even though he is an extrovert in his personal life. He is single and enjoys the opposite sex with no strings attached.

. . .

IVOR IS by himself and observing his counterparts, wondering when is a good time to slope off. He is standing next to a table which is waist-high. He has a glass of champagne in his hand. He notices Xavier walking in his direction and turns around to face away from him. He hopes that he will walk past him.

Xavier stands behind him and speaks, 'Ivor. Good to see you are here. I wondered if you were going to make an appearance.'

Ivor cringes before he turns rounds to face him; 'You requested my presence. Nice house and nice hospitality. Enjoyed the glazed lamb in honey. Different.'

Xavier finds him humorous as he says, 'Walk with me. I came over to ask if you are on board with us. You have been distanced from us.'

Ivor walks by his side. 'I have given you access to my company resources to support the cause. My business has been at your disposal. I assume you will have a safe house when things go south?'

Xavier chortles, 'Of course. Somewhere away from harm. As I said, a few weeks before we implement our plan, I will send the co-ordinates for you to fly to. Tomorrow's world will be here soon.'

Ivor does not show any emotion. 'What about children? Have you thought of that?'

Xavier has no solution. 'Some will survive like the rest of the humans. We will mould them.'

Ivor is keeping his cool. 'No one is safe. How are you going to change the world, let alone reconstruct it?'

Xavier has already accounted for that; 'We have a strategy in place. You don't need to know.'

Ivor slowly nods his head. 'Will The Order fund that? You're willing to use your own money to fund tomorrow's world?'

Xavier has another method; 'We are going to use tax-payers' money held in government bank accounts around the world to fund the new world.'

Ivor is interested in how the world will run, so he asks, 'And policies. Economy, education and trade deals?'

Xavier keeps his cards close to his chest. 'We will reveal that when the time comes. We will expect you to hold the purse strings. You will be the first global financial treasurer.'

Ivor has heard enough. 'Interesting. Well, I have to go now. I have a flight to catch back to Montenegro. I will see you again.'

Xavier shakes his hand and says, 'Thanks for coming. Will get back in touch.'

Ivor leaves the room and goes to the front door to leave.

. . .

IVOR HAS a driver waiting in the drive to take him to his plane. As soon as he is outside, he is keen to leave with his driver.

His driver knows what the meeting is about and asks Ivor, 'What happened in there?'

Ivor makes himself comfortable in the back of the limousine. 'It looks like it is happening in four months' time. I do not know how they are going to end the world. I do not know if the other families have been informed of the details. Whatever they have planned, it will be more devasting than World War Two.'

The driver is worried. 'What do you have planned if they pull this off?'

Ivor has no idea. 'They want me to be treasurer for the world. Ah. Crazy.'

The driver is curious; 'Will you try to find out and get help to stop it?'

Ivor can only think of one person. 'I don't know. I already told people in England. They have not done anything. No one has taken Jane Knight seriously. It has been four years since I first mentioned it. When we get back, I want to pack and find somewhere to go. I don't feel safe staying in Montenegro.'

XAVIER WALKS BACK to the rest of the guests. He takes a glass from a waiter walking with a tray towards him. He then goes to find someone else who was invited to the meeting. He is not related to the society, but he acts on their behalf. The man notices Xavier and waits for him to come up to him.

Xavier is keen to speak to him. 'Epson. Thanks for coming. Is everything in place?

Epson is admiring his house, staring at the ceiling and walls. 'Yes. There is about twenty million dollars in an account in her name. Ivor is looking after the account. It is ready to use to discredit Jane Knight. There is something that has bothered me these past three years.'

Epson thinks back to three years ago, 'How did you know that Ada would not kill her? She ended up going into a coma.'

Xavier thinks about the question before replying, 'I didn't. I was not expecting Ada to be there. I knew she wanted revenge and emailed her the name. She didn't say that she was going after Jane in Montenegro.'

Epson still has other questions; 'How did you know that, at some point, people may listen to Jane?'

Xavier wanted to cover all eventualities., 'I needed to make sure that if anyone began to believe in Jane, what better way to thwart that than to lose respect for her.'

Epson understands. 'So, why did you ask me here? We have never met in person before. We have always communicated via email.'

Xavier smiles and says, 'I wanted to make sure we are still on track. Ask in person. Have you crossed all the T's and dotted the I's?'

Epson gives him reassurance; 'All the money and accounts are in place. There is a little over a trillion dollars between the members. The success of Brexit helped provide half a billion dollars of that. I won't ask how you managed to instigate that.'

Xavier returns to Jane Knight. 'How soon can you give me copies of the transactions made in Jane's name? I want to pass the financial records and copies of the bank balance of twenty million dollars to MI6. I will give it to our spy inside The Agency.'

Epson explains what he has; 'I have kept all three years of multiple trade in the black market held on your blockchain in Switzerland. They give the names on accounts of buyers wanted by MI6. I can give the full history of exchanges between Jane Knight and the people most wanted. It will send her to prison.'

Xavier is pleased with his answer; 'Good.'

Epson changes the subject. 'What were you discussing in the meeting?'

Xavier refrains from telling him. 'Not of your concern. I hope I did not keep you waiting too long.'

Epson arrived halfway through their meeting. 'Didn't wait too long. Was not expecting dinner. One thing has popped into my mind. What do you want to do with the money? Once Jane is sent to prison, I mean.'

Xavier is not bothered, so he says, 'Do as you wish. We don't need it.'

Epson is rich enough and not motivated by greed. 'Just leave it in there for now. Ivor can do something with it.'

The conversation finishes and they join the rest of the party.


A FEW DAYS LATER, Xavier is walking outside by his pool. The steps from his house lead onto his patio where there is a large swimming pool. A few feet away from the pool is a patch of tall flowers that are planted in between the patio slabs. In amongst the slabs, there are rectangular holes that sit a foot apart from each other and are filled with compost for the flowers.

He prunes them in his spare time as a way of relaxing.

Beyond the swimming patio and swimming pool is lush grass making up the rest of his garden, which extends to one acre. Tall trees border the perimeter of his large backyard.

Today he goes to see if there are any leaves in the pool to let his gardener know to have a pool cleaner come in.

Xavier is wearing trousers and a short-sleeved shirt, untucked.

SOMEONE COMES out of his house and briskly walks down the steps to speak to him. It is one of the employees who assist him.

He is a tall man with long thick black hair that is combed back. He is Caucasian with a bronze suntan from living in Spain. He is in his thirties and wearing a beige two-piece suit with a tie and patterned shirt.

The man has an update for him.

XAVIER WONDERS what he has to say; 'What do you want?'

The man replies in a thick Russian accent, 'The new headquarters is fully operational now. It went live as of an hour ago. The society can move in anytime now.'

Xavier smiles with delight. 'Excellent. I will settle my affairs here and fly over within the week.'

The man is curious; 'Are you moving the schedule forward now?'

Xavier pauses for a moment, then says, 'No. One piece of software is still in need of correcting. It is also being held in another country. Once the problem is fixed, it will be flown to the new headquarters. I want to stick to September which will allow for plenty of time to move everything over.'

The man sounds content; 'That will allow for further testing when the problem is resolved. I have sent everyone the destination and co-ordinates. Like you asked, I have left Ivor out. I thought he was going to be treasurer after we take control of the world?'

Xavier explains, 'For a while, I have known that Ivor has been feeding information to The Agency, and hence why he has not been involved in the details of the operation. I have kept him alive because we still need him, unfortunately. His company is providing some of the components. But he will be part of the collateral damage.'

The man asks about the mole inside The Agency; 'What about the girl who has been working for us all along?'

Xavier walks over to his flower bed. 'I will have a helicopter pick her up when the time comes. By the time they realise she is the mole, it will be too late. Is there any other thing to discuss?'

The man tells him that is all but is hesitant. 'Why don't you just kill Jane Knight rather than waste time making her suffer?'

Xavier has his own reasons. 'She will die from the fallout, but I just want to toy with her in the meantime. But I have a group that is on standby if the plan fails!'

The man is confused, 'Why do you think the evidence of buying illegal guns will not work?'

Xavier likes to cover all angles. 'She has been in The Agency for five years. Her boss may find it preposterous, despite MI6 putting the case forward.'

The man asks, 'Are they already in England?'

Xavier smells one of the flowers and says, 'They will be. Our contact is monitoring her whereabouts. They have been since Ivor told her of our existence. We have people around the world that can stop her and Charles May if they get too close to finding out our plan, or should they scupper my plans to ruin her life. I want her suffering in prison a few months before September arrives.'

The man is finished giving him an update and heads back into the house, leaving Xavier alone.

**4**

# OPENING UP

It is the middle of the afternoon on Thursday. After we get back into the office from Shenzhen, we write up our report for the Foreign Secretary to use for his next meeting.

OUR OFFICE IS OPEN-PLAN, with Miles having his own office at the end. The office is busy, as usual, with colleagues coming and going.

We are in the middle of writing up the report on our last mission in China.

Our five-thousand-word report is almost finished and we are finalizing the findings. The report includes what we managed to retrieve and our hostile confrontation, including stealing a helicopter. I read out the notes I made while Charles types and includes other information I have overlooked.

Miles walks over to us to express his appreciation for our work. He says that our department has been praised by the Foreign Secretary as well, for showing that the Chinese company's technology is a risk to national security.

Charles and I see it as part of our daily work and so do not think any more about our assignment.

Miles still shows his appreciation even though we do not think anything of it.

When Miles walks back to his office, Stephanie comes over. She is the office manager who reviews reports before they go in front of senior staff.

She has always had an issue with me ever since I started working here.

Charles had a word with her and I had a final blow with her a couple of years ago.

Stephanie behaves like we are friends but I never acknowledge her presence. However, she is happy to pretend that we get along.

Stephanie does not spend too much time with us as we continue with our report, indicating we are busy.

WHEN WE FINALLY FINISH WRITING UP OUR last assignment, it is close to three o'clock and we wonder what to do for two hours. We have no new work for us to investigate. If there is no immediate trip to make, I think about us taking some time off and considering us for a change.

CHARLES LEANS BACK in the chair and stretches his arms in the air. He is glad to have finished typing and thinks about having some time off while it is quiet.

He has plans to formally introduce Jane to his parents, but is not sure if she is ready to meet the future in-laws.

He has temporarily made plans to see his parents for dinner tomorrow. He is prepared to go by himself if she is not ready to meet them yet, but he is confident that she will be happy to meet them again. They have never discussed the future due to work commitments.

CHARLES' thoughts move on to how much he enjoyed their quality time together in Shenzhen. He cannot think when they last had time together. He misses the time when they regularly made love. He feels in the mood to rekindle the old times tonight. He has plans to make dinner for Jane to get them in a romantic mood.

I CANNOT STOP THINKING about Shenzhen and how much I enjoyed our time together. I want to have a repeat tonight. I see Charles is tired as I watched him stretch. I hope he is up for round two tonight as I miss our intimacy.

BARNEY APPEARS out of nowhere and seems to want to talk to me, but he is anxious. He glances at Charles and I gather he wants to talk in private. I go to ask Charles to get us some coffee, but a colleague comes up to ask Barney for IT help. Barney smiles, disappointed, and I wonder what he wanted to talk about.

· · ·

THE LAST TWO hours drag by with three cups of coffee from the vending machine. When it is time to go home, Charles suggests going to his place instead of mine.

We order a taxi instead of using the underground to go home.

CHARLES' place is in Notting Hill, along Tavistock Road. We are having a dinner that he has prepared. It is rare that he cooks for me as we normally have a takeaway whenever we stay at his place. He has baked two whole rainbow trout with two thin slices of orange inside the filleted fish.

He has also steamed new potatoes with a side of salad.

While we have our dinner, I sense Charles wants to say something but he behaves weird. He is about to mention something then shuts down and eats.

I find Charles funny which irritates him as he finds it harder to tell me what is on his mind. I drink a glass of red wine to disguise my humour.

WHEN WE FINISH DINNER, I help with loading the dishes and cutlery into the dishwasher. As I go to switch it on, Charles wraps his arms around me from behind. I welcome his affection and I turn round to face him. We embrace in a kiss and we go into the living room.

I HAVE NEVER KNOWN us to be so intimate twice in one month. I wish we could do this three times a week.

I really want him inside me and making love to me tonight. Charles slides his hand inside my blouse and I feel his warm hands slide against my skin and reach my breast. I sigh and begin to get turned on by him caressing me.

It is not long before I feel him getting aroused as I rub him through his trousers to tease him. It makes me want him more. As I feel him getting hard, I want to make love. He always makes me reach ecstasy when he makes love to me.

I breathe heavily and tell him that I want him inside me. Charles does not need encouragement and we end up on the floor hastily pulling our clothes off. It is not long before I feel Charles slide himself into me and instantly feel myself getting wet. I swear he feels bigger since we last made love in China.

I can hear Charles releasing his pent-up sexual tension as he pushes hard inside me. I encourage him by wrapping my arms around his waist and pulling him towards me.

We kiss passionately like we have not seen each other in months. We struggle to catch our breath as we make up for the work-related lack of affection.

I find myself beginning to cum as his motion stimulates my sensitive area. It makes me force him to go harder to reach climax sooner.

Charles' breathing tells me that he is close to releasing himself also. Without warning, we both explode and lock ourselves together as our bodies cramp and stiffen. We both yell uncontrollably, letting out our sexual frustration.

WE BOTH BURY our heads into the others shoulder and laugh when we finish riding the crest of the wave. We cannot believe how much we needed that.

I feel my hair is soaked with beads of sweat and feel both of our bodies are clammy. Charles brushes my nipple and sends a shock through my body. It makes me realise how long it has been since I last felt my breast that sensitive after love-making.

CHARLES IS ALSO sensitive as he gently pulls out to reduce irritating his end. He also feels more cum leaking out as he exits. He admires Jane's body with a film of sweat accentuating her torso. He finds her breasts sensual as they gleam and sees that her nipples are still hard.

He watches Jane recovering and drifting in and out of sleep. He admires how cute her features are and feels compelled to press his lips against hers.

As I FEEL myself going to sleep, I sense Charles kissing me, which wakes me up, and I welcome the affection. It is not long before we have a shower.

AFTER WE SHOWER and dry ourselves, Charles finally tells me that he wants me to meet his parents a second time. I now realise why he behaved hesitantly earlier.

I first met them at a friendly football match between our Agency, MI5, MI6 and Government Communications Headquarters. They came with Charles to watch me play in the tournament. But I did not really have a chance to properly get to know them and we were not in a relationship then.

Now, he is ready for me to get to know them as his girlfriend. At first, I feel great about him seeing a future in us which I never doubted. In the next moment, I am taken aback and wonder why now, as we have been together for three years. I expected to meet his parents within a couple of years. We watch each other change into our nightwear as we talk about it.

Without notice, he tells me that we are going to see them tomorrow night for dinner. I had made no plans for myself or us but allow it all to sink in.

After we finish discussing it and expressing my views in regards to allowing myself to catch up, I welcome his gesture. Then we soon go to bed and drift off quickly.

I HAVE a vivid dream of being punched in the face and stomach by a woman called Ada, inside a boxing ring. I am trapped in the corner and cannot move. While I am dreaming, I feel my body is frozen and I cannot wake myself up.

The next second, I am against the rope without physically moving. She grabs my hair and wraps my long hair around the top rope. Then she hits me in the face repeatedly and there is nothing I can do.

Charles is standing below me watching helplessly as Ada is beating me to death. My dream suddenly changes and I am somewhere else I have been before.

I am in a football changing room that is at Hackney Marshes. I find myself in only my underwear in the dark. It is pitch black and I cannot see anything. I spin round hoping to see an exit or another person to help me.

Out of nowhere, I see a woman I recognise as Stephanie coming towards me from out of the dark and I begin to run. I feel like I am running on the spot and she is gaining on me. She grabs me and I scream as she has a hold of my neck and shoves me into a row of changing benches with clothes hooks. I go crashing into them and can feel the pain of my body crashing onto the corner of the bench. I find myself trapped underneath. Stephanie stands over me as I struggle to get from underneath the bench. Stephanie proceeds to punch me in the face repeatedly. I dream of blood seeping out of my nose and free-flowing as she continues to repeatedly hit me.

I BOLT upright in bed with a film of sweat around my neck and shoulders and my hair is soaked. I panic and quickly feel my mouth and nose as I mistake my sweat for a nosebleed. My body is shuddering from the nightmare and I breathe deeply from the bad dream.

I then panic that I have woken Charles, my boyfriend, from my knee-jerk reaction coming out of my subconsciousness.

I turn to him to check if he is awake but luckily, he is in his own deep sleep. I feel relieved that he did not see me having the same dream for the umpteenth time over the last six months, even though I had the two experiences three years ago. I find my side of the bedsheets drenched in my perspiration.

I then sigh as I realise it is only a dream and I need to get out of bed. I decide to get a glass of water from the kitchen.

Before I do, I quickly check that I am not bleeding as I feel my nose is really runny.

IN THE BATHROOM, I lift my head so I can see right up my nose in the mirror and check for a red colour. I give a huge sigh and bow my head, relieved that I have not messed the white sheets. I now go into the kitchen to get that glass of water.

I DO NOT KNOW why I have been having this recurring dream after so long. I know that it is caused by Post Traumatic Stress also known as PTS for short. It was brought on by my fight with Ada Mashkov, who died accidentally in Montenegro. She wanted revenge for her brother Vladimir's death. His body was never found.

She wanted to torture me slowly by forcing me to fight her in a boxing match. If it was not for the turnbuckle breaking from the force of me being repeatedly hit in the stomach, she would still be alive. Her punches to my body caused my back to slam against the turnbuckle and it eventually caved in. We both fell out of the ring and came crashing onto the concrete floor below. She landed on me and her forehead smacked on the floor and instantly killed her. It did not help that she had an underlying brain condition that contributed to her death.

WHILE I HAVE a glass of tap water, I stand against the kitchen counter. I notice the time on the oven and see it is after five in the morning.

I stare into space as I ponder on my recurring dream. I remember my shrink telling me that I would have these nightmares when confronting my issues. But I did not think it would feel real and raw.

I still see a shrink as a crutch to help me live a normal life. I am no longer suicidal because of Dr John Kavanagh's cognitive therapy. He has also made me feel myself again for the first time since childhood, and work colleagues, as well as friends, have seen a huge change in my personality. I have the self-confidence that I have never had for years.

I have my first long-term relationship with Charles May, and that is something that I never thought would happen in my life. I have also experienced my first love and lover.

While taking my time drinking my water at six o'clock in the morning, I appreciate how lucky I feel.


CHARLES APPEARS and wonders how long I have been up as he squints his eyes under the kitchen light. He is only wearing the bottom pants of his pyjamas, giving a view of his muscular chest. I can still not get used to his solid thick chest with a slight six-pack. His arms have definition and big biceps.

He rubs his eyes like he is a toddler who has just woken up and walks over to me for a kiss.

We linger for a while before we pull away and smile at each other.

Charles goes into the fridge to get a drink. 'Are you looking forward to seeing my parents again?'

I have not had a chance to really think about it, what with our trips. 'Yes. I remember them being very nice. Will they remember me?'

Charles gulps down his drink before answering, 'Of course they will.'

I wonder if they will like him seeing someone new. 'Will they be funny with you having a girlfriend since your wife's passing?'

Charles is not fazed by introducing me as his girlfriend, and continues, 'They knew that I would eventually find someone else. They know that I will never forget Naomi. You know how they were when I introduced you to them that day. They loved you.'

I wonder if it is because I was introduced as a work colleague. 'Yeah, but we were friends. We were not dating or going out with each other. Even though I fancied you from then.'

Charles smiles, 'You never told me that.'


I WAS into Charles the moment we first met when I had my training. 'I had no confidence to say I liked you back then.'

Charles remembers what I was like back then. 'I forget you were shy back then. I had no idea how much you liked me.'

Now, I can comfortably say, 'I fancied you from when I had my training after joining The Agency. I think I loved you from when we went on our first assignment.'

Charles appears stunned; 'You liked me all that time?'

I admit something else; 'I used to fancy Miles before I met you. He was the reason why I chose to join the new agency. I found out that he had a long-term girlfriend. He told me they were getting married. I even tried to end my life then, as well as that night before we went to the Caymans.'

Charles is more surprised. 'I never thought you two had something.'

I clarify how we were; 'It was one-sided. I thought he liked me when he was profiling me for the job. Made a fool of myself. Then you came along. And I fell in love.'

My thoughts go back to my dreams and Charles senses that something is bothering me. He does not know about my PTS as I have managed to hide the symptoms well.

Charles wants to know what is bothering me and coaxes me; 'Talk to me.'

I eventually open up; 'I have PTS, Charles.'

Charles is not bothered by my announcement. 'It doesn't change who you are. I'm still in love with the same person. How long have you had this?'

I am worried about his reaction. 'It started three years ago when we were on our second assignment.'

Charles knows when; 'That was when you had your fight with Ada. That fight was brutal. It scared me when I had to watch you taking those nasty punches. I'm not surprised that caused PTS. You almost died. Why couldn't you tell me back then? I wouldn't have judged you.'

I admit, 'I felt embarrassed. I still feel embarrassed. This doesn't happen to us. We always take a hit.'

Charles does not care. 'I don't respect you any less or see you as a victim. You don't think I struggled when I lost my wife? You think I moved on as normal?'

I cannot compare that. 'But you lost someone you loved. I did not lose anyone.'

Charles does not see it that way. 'Whether it is a loss of a loved one or directly hurt yourself, it is the same thing. Have you told your counsellor?'

I already told my therapist. 'He knows. But I only mentioned it recently. He is having me face it rather than run away from it. He prewarned me that I would have nightmares. But it is also part of the therapy.'

Charles is relaxed now that he knows I am dealing with it. I still do not feel any less embarrassed. Charles asks what kind of dreams I have been having.

I reluctantly describe them; 'There are two that merge into one. They both relate to the boxing fight and when Stephanie first gave me grief.'

Charles shows sympathy towards me, saying, 'I wish that it was me fighting Ada. I would have knocked her sideways. And Stephanie, I wish I had spoken to her sooner.'

That is what I love about Charles. We finish quenching our thirst and go back to bed for a few hours.

# 5

## A NEW ENEMY

A piece of land in the British Virgin Islands, near the Dominican Republic, is owned by an American financier. The land is in a time zone five hours behind Britain.

The island is two miles long and one and a half miles wide.

THE OWNER'S name is Epson Bernstein and he is an American in his fifties and is Caucasian. He has dark grey hair that is straight and thick. He is five foot seven with a slim build. He plays squash regularly, at his purpose-built court on his island, with the intention of keeping himself fit.

He wears plain short-sleeved shirts, untucked, with chino trousers.

EPSON GREW up in New York in the Bronx in a working-class family. His father worked as a cleaner and struggled to put food on the table. His mother earned little money as a seamstress altering clothes and ironing for wealthy couples.

His mother had to take him with her when he did not have school. He became fascinated by how the wealthy lived and told himself that he wanted to have the same lifestyle.

He did not resent his parents for not being able to give him nice clothes or presents. He dreamed of taking care of them one day when he had made his money.

When he finished school, he canvassed the neighbourhood selling goods stolen from warehouses; anything from electrical items to gadgets. He did not make much money from it.

One day, he overheard a commuter, on the train to Wall Street, talking numbers and saw from his clothes that he had money. He imagined being like him and sat next to him. The man wore an eighties' power suit with corporate button braces that the character Gordon Gekko wore in the movie "Wall Street".

After the man finished talking on his mobile, which was the size of a brick, Epson began asking him what he did for a living. He soon told him that he made his living trading with other people's money to get richer.

Epson lied to him saying that he was finishing college and thinking of going into finance himself. The man mentioned an internship, working for nothing but having invaluable experience. The man gave him a business card with the company name.

He found a way of getting someone to fake his qualification papers to get onto the internship. There, he used his selling technique, learned from door-to-door canvassing flogging knock-off goods.

Epson ended up getting an offer to work as a graduate but his stories were not consistent. Before being caught out, he applied for another job using the good name of his current employer. There, he began to make his money.

His work is trading in arbitrage on behalf of clients, buying and selling assets between markets and making money on the exchange rate. Assets also include currencies.

He made a killing when Brexit was announced, making close to twenty million dollars. His net worth is circa $250,000,000.

Epson has also been trading through cryptocurrency, as it is unregulated by any financial conduct authority, so, he can trade without being observed. He began trading through the unregulated market when he could make extra money trading on the black market.


THE ISLAND IS the holiday home that he visits regularly at the weekends and odd days during the week. He has a few permanent staff who live on the island and share the upkeep. They also know how to use discretion.

Epson also has certain friends, acquaintances and particular clients who come to the island for entertainment. He invites ten over at a time.

The entertainment takes the form of ten girls aged between eleven and sixteen years of age. They provide company to Epson's visitors, and services that include massages as well as anything else that his guests ask for. He has been offering entertainment for as long as he has owned the island.

The girls also stay on the island and are treated to activities in return for providing themselves to his visitors. They go on spa days, are taken to fancy clothes shops and showered with gifts like perfume and jewellery. But they have to wear them when they spend time with the next guest.

THE ISLAND HAS a white mansion with fifteen bedrooms and a study room on the ground floor. There is a pontoon in the shape of a horseshoe with a couple of small speedboats, which are used to get onto the main island. The front of the house faces the boats.

There are also a couple of white pool houses, situated around the island near the beach, that the girls use with the guests.

The mansion and the pool houses have hidden cameras in the bedrooms as well as around the island. There is a security room inside the mansion on the ground floor with a modern-day computerised system. You can see every inch of the island from the office.

Epson keeps a library of recorded activities in each bedroom, having clear footage of the guest's face. Digital video recordings of men with the girls are catalogued in the mainframe, inside the security room. They are kept as an insurance policy.

Drugs, such as cocaine and marijuana, are recreationally used by both the guests and the girls, as well as Absolut Vodka, Bacardi and Tequila.

The island has its own generator to supply light and heat.

EPSON ALSO HAS an English partner who is involved and helps to find new girls in the age range. They replace the girls that reach the age of eighteen when they are past their prime. They find new girls by encouraging the existing ones to approach girls on the mainland. They are promised fun, anything they desire and as many gifts as they want.

HIS PARTNER IS CALLED Dame Rochelle Klewer. She is in her early fifties with dark brown hair that is cropped and dyed to hide the few grey hairs. She has aged fairly well but has some wrinkles on her face.

She is five foot nine with pale skin and rosy cheeks with a glint of mischievousness in her eyes.

She grew up as a single child being spoilt by a wealthy family, and her parents are money-hungry.

HER FATHER OWNS A MEDIA COMPANY, selling magazines around the world, with offices in Europe, America and Asia as well as England.

Her parents' way of showing her love was to shower her with gifts and lavish activities to keep her amused.

Her mother only had interests in seeing her wealthy friends for spa days, afternoon tea and horse riding. She made no time for her daughter.

Her father travelled frequently between his offices, and so, was never around to give his attention to her. He also has various women in each city and was preoccupied with keeping them happy with his presence.

When Dame Rochelle reached adulthood, she turned to dabbling in cocaine out of boredom since she could have whatever she wanted. She has never needed to work and so she has no concept of a normal life.

She has grown up to be a narcissist, thinking that she can have anything she wants, and believing she has a right to it all.

Epson and Dame Rochelle met when she came to America to attend a socialite party. There was an instant attraction for one another. When she knew that he owned an island, she gave him the idea of making money palming girls off to his discreet friends. Dame Rochelle manages the girls as she does not have a job to go to.

They have been running the joint venture for ten years now. Their guests include a Judge from the mainland, American politicians, some of his investors and some oil billionaires from the Far East.

They make about ten thousand dollars a week.

The girls they find are all slim and of similar height, below six foot. They are a mixture of brunette, redhead and blonde girls. They all have long hair with similar features.

The girls are from privileged families that can afford to send their child to private school abroad. They are left to their own devices at such a young age. It is a game of chance that they know one of the girls who stay on the island.

For the majority of the time, they are lonely and miss home. Girls from the island promise them company and being offered nice gifts.

When they come to the island, Dame Rochelle sells the idea of being free to come and go to the island. She has them visit at weekends first and eventually, gets them to stay weeks at a time. The existing girls show them the ropes and explain that it is perfectly normal.

New girls are asked if they want to make easy money on the side, giving basic massages, which only involve the shoulders and back. They are slowly introduced to alcohol to make them feel relaxed and lose their inhibitions. Eventually, they are asked to massage the whole body, which then leads to intimacy.

They get a taste for the trappings and spoils and cannot leave. By the time they realise that it is not the fairytale of hanging out with rich people and being made special, they are too embarrassed to ask for help.

It is a conveyor belt to Epson and Dame Rochelle that works like a well-oiled machine.


IT IS after one o'clock in the morning on Friday and all the lights suddenly come on around the edge of the island. One of the girls has gone missing and the guest realises that he cannot find her.

He passed out from intoxicating himself with strong alcohol and white powder. When he came to, his girl for the weekend is not in his bedroom. He casually wanders the island trying to find her, thinking she is playing hide and seek. He finds it amusing at first, until an hour goes by and he has searched everywhere.

He raises his concern with Epson and he, in turn, goes to the security room by himself, telling his guest to go back to his room. Epson cannot find the girl on the CCTV cameras and thinks the worst. He gets all his staff, including Dame Rochelle, to search for her.


THE GIRL IS twelve years of age and her guest encouraged her to drink with him. When he passed out, she noticed white powder on the coffee table. She saw him earlier, sniffing the substance, and was told not to copy him.

She is too drunk and curious to reason why she should not smell the powder herself. Out of curiosity, she tries it, remembering how he inhaled it inside his nose.

After only a couple of tries, the strength is too much for her to cope with. She instantly gets a high and decides to go for a wander outside.


STAFF SCOUR THE ISLAND, shouting her name out as if she is past her curfew. Different voices are shouting into the pitch black, calling out 'Helen', but with no response.

After about half an hour, one of the staff notices a shallow hole in the sand filled with ocean water. There is about a foot of water with a body lying face down inside. He can make out that it is one of the girls and assumes it is Helen. He gets the rest of his colleagues' attention and they gather round the lifeless body.

Epson pushes through his employees to see for himself. He does not show sympathy like a normal person would. He sees the girl's body as an inconvenience and a stain on the carpet that needs to be removed. All he can think about is how soon he can get rid of the body before one of the guests contacts the police. He does not want the police finding out that he has a trafficking business on his island. He sees the dead girl as a loose end to be tidied to avoid attracting attention.

Dame Rochelle finally arrives and sees the concern on Epson's face. She can see that he finds the situation annoying, a bit like getting a parking ticket. She discretely stands next to him and both wonder how to dispose of the body.

Epson's staff know what their characters are like and can guess what the outcome will be.

EPSON AND DAME ROCHELLE are wondering if the staff are comfortable with disposing of the body without drawing attention to themselves.

Epson suggests that she ask some of his staff to take the body off the island. Also, to do it quickly before his guests realise it is a dead body being disposed of.

Three employees are asked by Dame Rochelle to use one of his two speedboats to carry the body and they are instructed to leave the body lying on the beach of the mainland at Charlotte Amalie and to make it appear that she had the accident there.

THE THREE STAFF leave her body a few feet away from the sea, so, it will appear that she had a misadventure swimming while intoxicated.

No one knows that she had snorted cocaine before tripping over into the hole.

THE NEXT DAY, Epson behaves like last night never happened. The dead girl's guest finds him and asks if she is okay. He lies saying that she had too much to drink and is now resting by herself in another bedroom. Epson is not concerned as his guest will be leaving the island today. The guest is hopeful to see her before he leaves and give her a gift. However, Epson does not raise his hopes and promises to pass the gift on to her. The man appears disappointed but accepts his response.

EPSON GOES into his study room to be by himself. Dame Rochelle finds him and asks if the two men have disposed of the body without being discovered.

He leans back in his chair behind his desk and motions yes. She is relieved that the problem is gone.

Epson is concerned that the parents will wonder what has happened to their daughter. He knows that the girls are encouraged to stay in touch with their parents, so as not to draw attention to their lucrative arrangement. Dame Rochelle is not fazed that their side business may come to light. She is confident that no one will give her death a second thought.

There is something else bothering him.

Dame Rochelle asks, 'What else is bothering you?'

Epson motions her to sit down. 'I know that nothing will come of this, but I have some clients who are obsessed with not having themselves attracting unwanted attention. They are a secretive bunch. Even though nothing will come of this, they may be twitchy and worried that this could bring them to light. They are quick to assume the worst.'

Dame Rochelle has never heard him mention these people before. 'Who are you talking about?'

Epson is cagey about his clients and answers without giving any detail; 'They like their privacy. That's all. You don't need to know any more.'

Dame Rochelle respects his confidentiality. 'How would they find out? It's not like they are watching you.'

Epson watches her chortle at the idea. 'I wouldn't put it past them. When I first met them, they were funny with how they met me. I was introduced by an intermediary. Never met the actual client.'

Dame Rochelle is puzzled; 'Seems sinister. How did you hear of them?'

Epson recounts, 'They found me. I didn't think at the time. I was making my first five million. Things were great. Assumed they were a referral. Never found out by whom.'

Dame Rochelle is curious and probes further, 'Who are they for you to be worried? The mafia?'

Epson sees that she is amused by her own comment. 'That would be easier. They would accept our extra-curricular activities.'

Dame Rochelle is not concerned. 'The guests are leaving today. We don't have any more till next weekend.'

Epson has other ideas. 'No. I think we should give it a couple of weeks before we have more guests. Wait to see what happens with the dumped body. You go to my place in New York. After we get rid of the visitors and the girls, you go. I have drinks in a couple of days for a new investment. I will catch up with you after that.'

The conversation finishes.

.   .   .

It is the middle of the afternoon and a young couple in their late twenties are going for a stroll along the promenade that leads to boulder rocks that break the waves, where the sandy beach ends.

They stop and lean on the chrome railing to look out at the ocean. They begin to canoodle when the girl catches an image out of the corner of her eye.

She makes a double-take and then tells her boyfriend that she thinks a body is lying against the foot of the rocks, on the edge of the beach where the water comes in. He tries to see what she is describing and then rushes over the railing, onto the sand. He thinks that she could be alive and he might be able to help her to the promenade.

When he reaches her, he realises that she is facing on her side, towards the rocks, and he turns her over. He sees that she is not alive and screams for his girlfriend to call the ambulance and police.

She frantically dials the number and watches her boyfriend in horror.

Ten minutes later, the police arrive and comfort the boyfriend, who is upset at what he witnessed. The girl is asked questions as to how they discovered the body. The ambulance finally arrives and the paramedics prepare to go out and collect the body.

It is not long before a small crowd forms, drawn by the commotion.

A detective arrives and sees the paramedics carrying away the deceased girl. He walks over to their ambulance and stops them from taking her inside.

He searches for any identification, including any coins or notes that a child would have on them. He finds nothing which makes him instantly suspicious. He knows he has nothing to go by for now and it will be a 'Jane Doe'. He wonders how long it will be before someone will come to the police station to report a missing girl.

# 6

## THE IN-LAWS

Charles drives us to see his parents in one of the hire cars that are randomly parked in the streets of London. During our drive there, we sit in comfortable silence and I stare out my window at the traffic.

I wonder what his parents' house will be like, where he grew up as a child.

CHARLES and I arrive at his parents' house at seven forty-five to have dinner at eight o'clock. I wonder if they will remember me from four years ago.

HIS PARENTS LIVE IN HARROW, outside of central London. Charles is an only child and his parents' home has lots of pictures of Charles with his parents. His parents also have their wedding photo in pride of place. They have their photos on a decorative brass trolley for aesthetic appearance.

HIS PARENTS' home has dark red carpets, in the hallway and upstairs, that seem to be from the eighties. The house is really lived-in with old ornaments relating to Guyana, where his parents are originally from. I see a black fabric that is like a scroll with a gold embroidery of Guyana. I feel that I am with a close family, deeply grounded in heritage.

The walls are covered in aged magnolia paint as if they came originally with the house. The ceiling is also a dull white. Even the white skirting boards have a tinge of yellow from age. I feel that the house has seen a lot of love.

I FOLLOW Charles into the dining room where his parents have already laid the table out with mixed white rice and kidney beans in a glass Pyrex, roast lamb on a metal tray, sweet potato, roast potatoes, broccoli, carrots and coleslaw in separate Pyrex bowls. The food smells really nice.

They have a cabinet that is almost the length of the wall it is against, with glass doors along the front. The cabinet houses their glassware, such as champagne flutes, wine glasses, decanter and china pots. On top of the cabinet are more photos, that also include a picture of Charles and his late wife Naomi. I am surprised it is not a wedding photo.

We sit down together and wait for his parents to come in so we can eat. We do not have to wait that long before they come in. Their names are Algernon and Abigay.

CHARLES' parents sit at opposite ends of the small oval-shaped dining table. His mum, Abigay, says a short prayer for the lovely meal they have prepared.

HIS MUM IS BUXOM, like a traditional Caribbean woman, and is in her seventies. She appears introverted and quiet. His dad is tall and slim with light grey afro hair and he is clean-shaven. He also seems reserved, with not much to say.

His dad is wearing a white and black checkered shirt with a maroon cardigan and brown cord trousers. His mum is wearing an old-fashioned dress from the eighties, that still fits her well, and it is covered with a floral pattern.

I can see that Charles looks more like his mum with a bit of his dad.

SOON AFTER THE PRAYER, Abigay hurries us to help ourselves to the prepared meal before it goes cold. While I help myself to the vegetables, Abigay begins to ask me questions.

She helps herself to the lamb as she talks; 'Charles tells me that you have been dating for three years.'

I have to finish what I am eating before I reply, 'Yep. Just over three years now.'

Abigay has an intense expression as she listens, then asks, 'How did you meet?'

I wonder if Charles ever talks to them about me. 'We met through work. I believe I met you just before dating Charles. He invited you to a mini football tournament.'

Abigay recollects, 'Oh. Yes, I remember now. You're the one who I saw that day. For some reason, I thought you were someone else.'

I chortle as she remembers. 'We were just work colleagues then. We didn't really know each other. We got together soon after that day.'

Abigay feels embarrassed and quickly asks about my background. 'Where are you originally from?'

I happily tell his mum, 'Milton Keynes. My siblings are still there.'

Abigay asks how many siblings I have and about my parents. Charles interrupts to explains on my behalf that my parents died. His parents show empathy and ask how long ago. I can now talk about it without being emotional, explaining that it happened four years ago and that it was a plane crash.

Abigay quickly moves on about work. 'So, you are a civil servant as well.'

I stare at Charles for an answer but he shows a blank expression. 'Huh, yeah. I'm not sure if you know exactly what Charles does, but we write reports and travel quite a lot.'

Abigay does not show any confirmation. 'What reports do you write?'


I GLANCE at Charles again for an answer but he does not make eye contact. 'Well, I write about companies. Ones that may be of interest to the government.'

Abigay still does not express an interest. 'Are you enjoying what you do?'

I try to make it more interesting, 'Work can be a killer. Certain companies we report on want to shoot you... us down in flames. The hours can be murder. But we get to close down businesses that are trading illegally.'

I notice Algernon is happy listening to us rather than interacting in our conversation.


WHEN WE FINISH DINNER, his mum begins to clear the table for dessert. She has made apple pie with custard.

Algernon now wants to make conversation. 'Where do you live, Jane?'

I assume he knows London fairly well, so I say, 'In Hackney, in an apartment that overlooks Homerton Overground.'

Algernon is thinking if he knows where that is; 'How far is that from London Olympic Park?'

I gauge how far it is to walk then reply, 'It is about a thirty-minute walk along Homerton High Street.'

Algernon pictures what I have told him. 'Okay. So, are you thinking of moving in?'

I have not even thought about it. 'We haven't discussed it. Not really crossed our minds.'

Charles thinks about it; 'I don't know why we have not talked about it. Work has been a distraction.'

I wonder if Charles will mention it or wait for me to bring it up. 'I'm sure we will now have a conversation about it, now you have brought it up.'

Algernon is neither surprised nor does he have an opinion. 'Which house will you move into?'

Charles sees that I am leaving that question to him, so he says, 'Well, it will be based on which place is bigger. I think my place has slightly more room. Also, it depends if Jane has a preference.'

I agree with him; 'I'm happy either way. So long as we are living together.'

Charles' mum comes back into the room with apple pie in a flat ceramic round pie dish with crinkle sides. It smells delicious and my mouth is watering. She also brings in a big jug of custard and my eyes pop out. I am now envious of his parents.

None of us says anything as we are enjoying his mum's apple pie. I take two helpings after his dad only has to ask me once.

My stomach is now truly stuffed and I feel like undoing the top two buttons of my jeans. When we are finished, his mum thinks out loud that she will start washing the dishes. I naturally offer to help his mum and we both collect the empty bowls and take them into the kitchen.

WHILE WE FILL THE DISHWASHER, Charles and his dad stay in the dining room. I sense Abigay wants to continue asking me questions about our relationship. She is hesitant to start the conversation.

I break the awkwardness by making a point; 'I notice that you have a photo of Charles and Naomi in the dining room. She was really attractive. I wish I could be that attractive.'

Abigay smiles at my comment. 'She had a nice personality to boot. I miss her and I think Charles misses her as well.'

I do not doubt that. 'Of course. I would never expect you two to forget her.'

Abigay asks me about how serious we are; 'Where do you see you two going?'

I have an idea, so I tell her, 'I would like to one day have children and change jobs so I am there for them. I imagine Charles being the father.'

Abigay is reserved; 'Charles went through hell when he lost his wife. I do not think he is ready to settle down with another girl.'

I feel that I am not worthy of Charles. 'I'm not trying to replace Naomi. I would never assume to replace her. Our relationship is different. No comparison.'

Abigay is hesitant again when she asks me a personal question. 'When you grew up, did you imagine yourself choosing a black man to settle down with?'

I feel caught off guard and taken aback. 'I didn't even think I would actually find someone who would want to go out with me, never mind thinking I would end up falling for someone. I do not see his skin colour. I see his character and his morals.'

Abigay now feels like she has offended me. 'I didn't mean it like that. I mean, Charles has never brought a white girl to our house before. They have always been black girls. His father and I are a bit surprised. That's all.'

I totally get where she is coming from. 'I can see why you would be shocked. I asked Charles if he had been with a white woman before. But I asked out of interest, not curiosity. I wondered what he saw in me. I have never been in a relationship with a white person. All I know is Charles.'

Abigay finds my response refreshing. 'How did you know that Charles was the one?'

I think back; 'I have a past that Charles found out about. But he saw past that and made me feel that it was okay. Despite my faults, he chose me because of my views and morals. He did not see my skin colour. That's how I knew he was for me.'

Abigay touches my hand as I dry a plate that cannot go in the dishwasher. 'I can see how much you make my son happy. He never invites a girl unless he really likes her.'

It means a lot for me to hear that, especially from his mum. Eventually, Charles comes in and interrupts us. He asks what we are talking about and we both smile at each other, leaving Charles to guess.

Soon after I finish helping his mum tidy the kitchen, Charles and I go home.


It is after ten o'clock When we get back to his flat, we relax in his living room. I flake out on his sofa and think about what his mum said about being the first woman he has dated. I question myself about why I ended up being his choice as a long-term girlfriend. I would never have thought he would choose me to have a relationship with. Looking back, I do not know why I have not asked him; why me? He could have had any woman but he chose me.

CHARLES SEES me deep in thought and sits on the edge of the sofa against my torso. He then leans over me and asks what is on my mind.

I find myself asking the question I have always wanted to know, 'What do you see in me?'

Charles smiles, not knowing where this is coming from. 'What has brought this up? Did my mum say something?'

I adjust myself to face him properly before answering, 'No. Your mum got me thinking. I have no idea what you see in me.'

Charles goes on the defence, standing up and walking away. 'What do you see in me? I lost a wife. A wife I would still be with if she was alive. I wouldn't look at another woman.'

I do not think he is being fair, 'No. No. I would not for a second have come on to you. It would not have been my first thought let alone my second. So, that does not count. I never asked you what you see in me.'

Charles faces me and I see his mind taking its time, 'Okay. I will tell you. Just give me a second. I do not want to get this wrong. I see you as the girl next door and extremely pretty. I love the way you are clumsy, with no commonsense, but intelligent at the same time. I love the way you are attentive towards me; the way you touch my hand whenever you can. I love the way you smile. I love the freckles on your face that accentuate your cute nose. I love the way you twirl your hair when you are deep in thought, like you're doing now. I love the way you show your weakness but are not ashamed. I love the way you look at me like I am the only person in the room. Is that enough?'

I find myself not playing with my hair and struggle to gaze into his eyes. I am lost for words as I did not expect those words to leave his lips. I had no idea that he felt so strongly about me.

Charles is still waiting for me to reply and I quickly conduct myself in a serious manner and begin thinking. Charles glares at me impatiently.

I find myself standing up and pacing around as I think methodically what I want to say, making sure that it is concise and in the right order.

I eventually face Charles as I clasp my hands together. 'Please don't laugh at me. I'm trying to be serious here. You ask me what I see in you. Well, like you said, I want to get this right.'

Charles crosses his arms trying not to laugh at me.

I point my finger at him; 'Right. I have it.'

Charles interrupts, 'You have no idea. You lecture me and you cannot say one nice thing about me. Do you love me?'

I snap at him, 'Of course I love you. There are so many things that I want to say but I don't know where to begin.'

Charles is growing impatient. 'I will go to bed. You stay here and think of what it is you like about me. Sorry, love about me. I will see you in the morning to hear your answer.'

I shush him while I point my finger at him. 'I love the way you have not forgotten your wife. I love the way you are able to love again, even though it hurt like hell in the beginning. I love how, out of all the people you could have, I am the only one you want to be with. I love the way you protect me and stand in front of me to shield me. I love the way you look at me. I love the way you touch me, hold me. I love the way you stare into my eyes like you have seen me for the first time. I love the way your forehead crinkles when you are deep in thought. I love the way you snore; it soothes me to sleep knowing that you are next to me.'

Charles resents that and quickly responds, 'I do not snore.'

I smile and walk up to him with nothing between us. 'I love the way you make me smile. I love the way how you make me be myself. I love the way you kiss me.'

Charles puts his arms around me, 'What else?'

I try not to giggle, 'I love the way you make love to me.'

Charles tries to keep a serious face, 'What else?'

I struggle to think of anything else, 'Umm. I love the way you asked me to marry you. When the time comes.'

Charles is taken aback and lingers over me, 'I love the way you said yes. When the time comes.'

We go quiet and gaze into each other's eyes. Then we kiss passionately like it is the first time. I think we just became engaged without expecting it.


WHEN WE GET inside the bedroom, we fight to take our clothes off and jump into bed. We grab hold of each other so tightly that we squeeze the air out between us.

I begin to arouse him by squeezing his manhood for a split second before releasing, to turn him on. I hear him quietly groan to himself as he likes the way I grab him with my hand.

When I know he is ready, I get on top of him and feed him inside me. I gasp as I forget how much deeper in he goes inside me when I am on top. I almost cum as he fully inserts himself inside me.

As I find the intensity stimulating my G-Spot, I go faster and harder to reach ecstasy quickly. I feel Charles flex his hips to push as far as he can go to reach the same place as me.

I cannot help myself groaning out loud as I lose myself in my own world. I am now feeling a wave coming on as I am so close to cumming. I squeeze my eyes as I breathe heavily waiting for my body to explode.

I eventually yell out as my body stiffens and I collapse onto Charles' chest. I begin to laugh not quite believing how much he made me orgasm. He thinks I have had a heart attack and checks that I am okay.

He jokes that he has not been given a chance to have his. I raise my head up to make eye contact and tease him that I have had mine and now I'm ready to go to sleep. He stares at me like he has been short-changed. I quickly put him out of his misery and tell him that he can get on top.

AS WE MAKE LOVE a second time, I cannot help think out loud, 'We fit together. We are one.'

Charles thinks the same; 'We are like chess pieces on a board. We go together.'

WHEN WE FINISH MAKING LOVE, I snuggle my back up against him with his arms around me as we fall asleep. His soft snore soothes me to sleep.

# 7

# FITTING PIECES TOGETHER

It is eleven o'clock on Saturday morning and a charter boat, arranged by Epson, arrives and moors along the pontoon to collect his guests. Dame Rochelle and Epson walk them to the boat and watch them board. The guests thank them for a relaxing weekend.

A COUPLE OF HOURS LATER, Dame Rochelle attends to the girls to prepare for their departure. She provides them with a plain cream envelope with money inside for each of them. She praises their efforts in providing everything the guests asked for. She gives them $1,000 each which is like $10,000 to a girl.

A few girls who know Helen wonder where she is and ask Dame Rochelle. She says that Helen is still recovering from a hangover. The girls are too young to be suspicious or question the response.

The girls are taken on two of the speedboats by Epson's two staff. They take them to a secluded part on Charlotte Amalie, so no one can see them come from the island. Once there, they put them in pre-arranged taxis to take them back to school.

EPSON WAITS with Dame Rochelle in his living room for the speedboats to return. They reaffirm their arrangement but she wants to stay with him. She wants both of them to leave together but Epson insists that he will follow behind her in a few days. She begrudgingly goes along with his plan.

Eventually, his employees arrive back and he asks them to take Dame Rochelle to the airport.

THE ISLAND FEELS like a ghost town with a skeleton staff. Epson lets the majority of his employees go home, leaving a drinks server, a canapé server and a general servant.

When the cocktail party is finished, he will let the remaining staff leave.

THE NEXT DAY, Epson walks through his house carrying a financial newspaper, a local paper and a cup of coffee. He is wearing a pair of beige chinos and a dark brown long-sleeved shirt, buttoned up to the top.

Epson walks towards the rear of the house through his patio door, to a large sandstone patio. He takes a seat at his round six-seater patio dining table. Epson reads the paper while sipping his mug of white coffee.

The New York Financial Times shows data on the NYSE. It is another sunny day with blue skies. He has no itinerary to follow and chooses to have a lazy day.

Dame Rochelle texted him when she reached his apartment and sees another text come through. They send messages to each other discussing their next group of guests and girls. She is keen to continue. Epson is still cautious about resuming their arrangement too soon, both from the point of view of the dead body being found, and his client learning about the incident. He thinks about pushing it back a month.

This is her only enterprise and she has no other interest.

After he finishes his conversation with Dame Rochelle, he anxiously opens the local paper to see if there is any report on the dead girl.

Epson opens each page as if he is peeling away a bandage carefully. Eventually, he finds a one-page article reporting a body found. He reads the story carefully to find out if they have identified the body. There is a telephone number to call which makes Epson feel relieved. It is likely that the police will never find the identity and Epson is confident of that.

WHILE EPSON TURNS the page over, he hears a helicopter and sees it appear from behind his house, a few feet above the roof.

He tries to see who is in the rear but the sun's reflection on the glass distorts his view.

After a few seconds, the pilot flies over his house again towards the pontoon. Epson places the newspaper on the table and walks around the side of the house from the patio area, along a single stepping-stone path with shrubs on either side.

THE HELICOPTER LOWERS onto the pontoon and gently lands. The down-draught causes the water to ripple and the two speedboats to rock a little.

The man in the rear waits for the top rotors to slow down before stepping out of the helicopter.

Epson walks onto the pontoon, a few feet clear of the rotating blades. One of his staff walks out of his house to accompany him.

THE MAN IS Caucasian in his early forties with fair skin. His face is slim and oval and he is clean-shaven. His hair is light brown, short and straight with a side parting. He is six foot tall with a slim build.

He is wearing a two-piece chocolate brown suit and a white shirt. His shoes are leather loafers.

He is Spanish with a soft accent and speaks fluent English.

His personality is calm and collected.

He works for The Order as their problem-solver. Any issues that could expose the organisation involve him making damage limitations.

He has been working for them for a number of years.

EPSON HAS MET him a few times and knows him as Lucas. Lucas has visited him a few times in the past, regarding his various inside trading deals. Epson has drawn attention to himself in business magazines with his short-term investment returns.

Lucas is already aware of the dead girl and has come to find out how a twelve-year-old ended up being on his island.

EPSON KNOWS why he is here but does not know how he found out so quickly. He tells his servant to get some more drinks while he walks Lucas back to his patio.

THEY BOTH TAKE A SEAT, a couple of chairs apart, and Epson waits for Lucas to make conversation first.

His servant arrives quickly with a fresh pot of coffee. They wait until he walks away so they can talk in private.

Lucas does not waste time; 'My people have heard that you had a girl die here.'

Epson does not feel nervous as he finishes pouring the coffee. 'Who gave you information about someone dying on my island?'

Lucas takes a sip of his coffee and stares into it as he answers; 'We have someone that works for you. He feeds us information as and when it is necessary. We have known about your side business for years. We were not interested as you yourself would want to avoid the attention. But a dead body? Now that is a reason for concern.'

Epson reassures him by showing him the local paper. 'Take a look on page six. They are appealing for anyone to come forward. Her parents do not live over here. The police here are not the type to publicise this around the world.'

Lucas is not too convinced. 'She went to a private school, All Saints Cathedral School. Rich parents take their kids there. They will eventually look into their missing child.'

Epson is confident that the death of the girl will not come back on him. 'When they identify the body, they will not trace it back to me. She was not found here. We are miles from Charlotte Amalie.

Lucas feels that he is over-confident. 'Well, I came here to tell you to shut down your operation. We cannot afford another dead girl. I suggest you try using adults. They will be able to handle their alcohol.'

Epson briefly thinks about his agreement with Dame Rochelle. 'We will make sure that we are more vigilant.'

Lucas needs to make himself much clearer; 'Let me make myself clear. We do not agree with your antics. We find out that you are continuing, we will let you go.'

Epson does not find him a threat, so he adds, 'I will take your thoughts into consideration. Now, I have a prior engagement. Please stay and finish your coffee. You can show yourself out.'

Epson leaves and goes back inside his house. He goes to his study room and phones Dame Rochelle.

Lucas calls his contact to give him an update. 'Hello. Spoke to Epson. It does not appear that he will rethink his enterprise. I think we need to take action.'

The man on the other end of the call agrees with him and wonders what he suggests.

Lucas sips his coffee then says, 'I think we should kill him. I will have something arranged.'

The person gives him the go-ahead and leaves him with the responsibility of deciding how Epson will be dealt with.


A COUPLE OF DAYS LATER, the dead girl's body is released to the coroner and an autopsy is carried out to establish how she died.

The examination is carried out by the local pathologist and he finds a few samples.

The first sample is a speck of leaf combed from her hair that he puts in a specimen container.

The second sample is sand found under her fingernails.

The third sample is sea water found in her mouth that he syringes and squirts into another specimen container.

The fourth sample is a speck of white substance inside her nasal passage and he uses a medical cotton bud that has a self-seal lid to collect it.

When he is finished with his findings, he jet-washes her body in preparation for opening her up. He does not find any marks on her body or head to suggest she was attacked. There are no marks around her neck. He can only deduce that she died by misadventure or self-infliction.

After opening her up, he checks her stomach contents.

The fifth lot of samples are shrimps, not fully digested, olives, tomato, cheese, caviar and alcohol.

After he is finished with her internal organs, he sews her up and leaves her as he found her.

He sends the leaf, sand, sea water and white substance off to forensics for analysis.

When he is finished, he puts her in a refrigerated mortuary to be kept there until someone can identify the body.

The body will stay with the coroner for a month before it is buried in an unknown grave, paid for by the state of Charlotte Amalie.


BACK IN ENGLAND, it is after nine o'clock at night. Barney is at home in the spare bedroom where he has a complete 'Crazy Wall' of who he thinks are members of The Order. The crazy wall has a number of sticker notes, newspaper clippings and magazine cut-outs of various people.

He has gone through business magazines such as Forbes, Platinum Business and Fortune to put a face to a name.

He also has strings pinned on the wall to show links between the various people on the wall.

He is confident that he has found all of them. They number twenty-one people, heads of their families, who are a part of the society. He knows what countries each family is living in and what companies they own. He suspects that someone by the name of Xavier Hark controls the group.

Barney has been using his work computer and connecting to the work server to gather the intel. He now wants to tell someone about the group. His manager, Miles, and head of The Agency, Mary, do not encourage the pursuit of The Order. Also, he wants to prove, with evidence, Jane's belief that the organisation exists.

He built up the crazy wall on the odd weekend and weeknight when he had no commitments, otherwise, he would have completed sooner.

HE BEGAN his search by using Vladimir Mashkov as a starting point, as Jane found out from a source that he was accused of being a member of The Order. He dissected Vladimir's business empire and listed business offices, warehouse sites and then directors, Chief Executive Officer and Chairman.

He remembers, from a passing conversation with Jane Knight, that Xavier Hark and Svana Chase were also linked to The Order. So, he wondered if any of them had ties with Vladimir or his management team. He found that some of them had ties with them.

After he found a connection, he gathered information on Xavier and Svana to see what their backgrounds were. He saw who they had links with and added them to the crazy wall.

Once he exhausted every avenue, he came to the conclusion that there could be a maximum of twenty-one groups of participants. He realised that they are potential families. He also thought that they dated back to sometime in the early 1900s. He has had to make some speculations with the information he found.

On a separate note, he has a dismantled smart box that he has been toying with. He senses that it is something to do with Vladimir but has no idea what. He has pulled apart the components inside the casing, loosening the wires and examining the chips on the motherboard.

It is left lying on his desk in exactly the same state as when he last tinkered with it.

HE IS MENTALLY DRAINED HAVING SPENT three years, on and off, and in his spare time, gathering the information. He sits in his chair and leans back with a glass of red wine. He wonders whether to show his girlfriend his work and asks himself how to approach his boss, Miles Stone.

As he thinks of her, he hears her knock on the door and ask if he is okay. He speaks out loud to ask her to come in. She checks if he is okay with coming in before slowly entering with a mug of tea. She has not been in their spare bedroom for months.

Kate is overwhelmed by how much detail he has on the wall. She asks how long it has taken him to compile all the data.

Barney is too tired to reply as he drinks his full glass of wine. He explains that he will have to report his work to his employer. Kate is too overwhelmed to hear what he said.

She has no understanding of his work but is fascinated with how he managed to prepare all this. He begins to deflate as he thinks back to when he first began his mammoth task.

They go into the kitchen to continue their conversation.


BARNEY AND KATE sit at their small two-seater table. He leans forward towards Kate and stares into his half-empty glass of wine and stirs the liquid around. Kate asks him what he is going to say to his manager. He is more curious about how they will react when he proves that Jane is right about investigating The Order. But the problem is explaining how they are a threat. He has not worked out what their agenda is. But his gut feeling is telling him that something bad is going to happen. He has a theory about what The Order may be planning. He senses that they are close to executing their plan in the not-so-distant future.


KATE SUDDENLY HOLDS HIS HANDS, holding the wine glass, encouraging him to report what he has found so far. She feels that his gut feeling is likely to be true. She asks if there is anyone he can talk to first for encouragement.

Barney has someone in mind who will believe him and so back him up when he goes down the official channel to report his findings. It is not Jane as she is busy travelling the world and buried under too much paperwork to find the time to listen. It will be Stephanie that he will tell and Kate encourages him to tell her sooner rather than later.

Kate notices that there is something else bothering him as she knows him so well. She naturally asks him what is occupying his mind. Barney hesitates at first, like he has a confession to make. Eventually, he says what is on his mind and tells her that he also discovered something else.

Barney explains that Vladimir had two people working for him and used The Agency software to locate their financial records. He saw that the last time they used their bank card was four years ago. They paid for a flight ticket. Barney clams up as he is about to tell Kate. She squeezes his hand again for reassurance. He finally continues saying that the flight resonates with him and began to bother him at the time. So, he explains that he looked at the manifest of passengers that were on the same plane as the two people. He came to realise that he recognised two other people that were on the plane. It dawned on him why he knew the information about the plane.

Kate is open-mouthed and says straight away that he has to tell the person what he knows. No matter how much it will hurt them, they deserve to know the truth. Barney does not argue with her but he does not know how he will tell the person.

It is now close to midnight and, on that note, Barney does not know how he is going to sleep now, as telling Kate makes it real.

# 8

## A FAVOUR

It is Monday morning and we are finished having our shower and putting on our work clothes. I'm wearing a pair of slim-fitting suit trousers and a plain white double-cufflink blouse. Charles is wearing his usual light grey three-piece fitted suit with a corporate diagonal stripe tie.

We take the underground train to travel to work.

WE ARRIVE in the office a little after nine o'clock. There is not much to do today with no reports to write up and no new assignment. Charles plays a card game on his computer while I catch up on old emails, deleting junk mail and irrelevant inbox messages. My fingers are getting cramped as I have over a thousand of them to go through. A lot of them are responses to original emails on politics in the office. That is one of the good things being in the field; you do not have to get involved in moans and groans about milk in the fridge, photocopier paper and missing yoghurt.

HALF AN HOUR LATER, Miles walks over to us and asks for us to come to his office. Charles quickly exits the application on his desktop.

Miles does not give a reason when he asks us to follow him. Charles and I glance at each other with curiosity, before following him into his office.

MILES ALREADY HAS a man in his office which makes us wonder why he has asked us in. The man is Caucasian and appears to be in his late forties with thick hair combed into a side parting. He is clean-shaven with very fair skin. His height is less than six feet tall and he is filled out a little.

His posture is authoritative with an aura of despair. He seems to be at his wit's end and gives a sigh of relief when Miles introduces us.

Miles shows reassurance with his introduction; 'These are my best field agents. I give you Charles May and Jane Knight. This is my old uni friend, Gordon Wrex. We were flatmates when we were students.'

Charles shakes his hand first. 'What do you do for a living?'

Gordon plays down his role, 'Just a civil servant to my constituents.'

Charles understands what he is saying. 'Ah, a politician. Maybe you can fix my parking tickets.'

Miles interrupts, 'He is kidding. Aren't you, Charles?'

Gordon turns to me, 'And you are the accountant. I heard so much about you with your theories. So, you cook the books.'

I try to be amusing, 'I cook buildings and cars now.'

Gordon gives a half laugh; 'Of course. So, you won't be able to fiddle my taxes.'

I smile at his comment. 'I could, but I wouldn't want you to get in trouble with the expense scandal.'

Miles laughs nervously, 'Right. Shall we discuss why you have come here?'

Gordon faces his worries again; 'I don't know where to start.'

Miles acts as an intermediary. 'From when you last spoke to your daughter.'

Gordon begins to recall his knowledge as he thinks deeply; 'I sent my daughter, Helen, to the Virgin Islands to be educated. She went to All Saints Cathedral School. She was in regular contact with her mother until about two weeks ago. After not hearing from her, we tried to call her. But her mobile is switched off now.'

I instinctively want to know her age. 'How old is your daughter?'

Gordon gets upset. 'Excuse me. She is twelve.'

I help give him hope; 'We can track her last known mobile location. Find out where her known location is, even if the phone is switched off.'

Charles continues, 'We can head over there and speak to the local police for any reports of a missing girl.'

Gordon appears more relaxed. 'That would mean a lot. If it helps, I can pay for your travel expenses.'

Charles glances at Miles, 'That won't be necessary. Miles can put it under The Agency expenses.'

I have one question; 'Why have you come to us? We deal with illegal companies.'

Miles answers the question, 'Excuse me, Jane. Gordon felt that he could come to me to look into it. I thought it would be better if I sent my best agents.'

I quickly remember the mobile; 'Can you give us your daughter's number?'

Gordon is puzzled and asks, 'Don't you need to know the make of the phone?'

I respond quickly, 'No.'

At this point, Miles asks Gordon to leave and he will meet him by the lift. He wants to have a word with us without Gordon here. Gordon gives us his daughter's number before he leaves.

Charles watches Gordon walk out and then turns to face Miles. 'Why us? This is a recovery mission. She is likely to be dead.'

Miles knows he is right but explains, 'I want a reliable source to confirm her death. That way, I can put him at rest and hopefully bring the body back to England for burial.'

Charles asks the same question, 'Why us? This is a Scotland Yard gig. Not our agency.'

Miles reiterates, 'You're the only two I can trust to do a good job. You will solve this in two days tops. Scotland Yard will bumble their way through. We have the technology.'

Charles sighs, 'When do you want us to get started?'

Miles hints that he wants us to leave now; 'You have a few days of nothing to do. You can see this as a vacation.'

Charles thinks more into it; 'What if we come up against resistance?'

Miles does not mince his words; 'You have diplomatic immunity. You do what you do best and kill 'em.'

I can see that this is not going to be a straight forward reconnaissance. 'I feel that we may face hostility. Will this affect relations between the British government and America?'

Miles does not care about that. 'There is already a strain. A British girl has gone missing on American soil. Just find the body, bring it back and then go on to your next assignment.'

We have no more discussion and so we leave his office and pack up our desks before heading out.

Miles catches up with his friend at the lift and escorts him out of the office.


I GO on my computer to book our flight for Charlotte Amalie tomorrow. The flight takes eight and a half hours.

Once I have our flight paid for, I search for hotels that will not be far from the police station and possibly the school she went to.

Charles thinks that the police will have a 'Jane Doe' body at the coroners. I tend to agree with him even though we do not want to be right.

Now both the flight and hotel are organised, I realise that we do not have a photo of her. Gordon is no longer here. The next best thing is social media and there cannot be too many surnames by the name of 'Wrex'.

It takes a while to search for her details and verify the right person, but we finally get there and I print out a picture of her as well as taking a picture on my mobile.

Our next task is to find out when she last had her mobile phone switched on and which tower it pinged from. We use Barney to help us find out.

BARNEY SEEMS to be distracted while he is gazing at his computer. Charles waves his hand behind his monitor to get his attention.

Normally, we have a catchup of what both of us have been up to and I ask how his girlfriend Katherine is.

Barney flickers his eyes like he is snapping out of a trance. He apologises like he has done something wrong and details out where he is with his work.

I ask if he is okay as I half laugh, lightening the mood. He waves his hand to change the subject.

Barney avoids contact with me. 'What can I do for you?'

Charles takes charge and asks, 'Can you trace this number to see when it was last activated and where?'

Barney taps a few keys before a field comes up to type the number in. 'Can I have the number?'

I have the number and pass it to him instead of reading it out, 'Here. The number is on the bit of paper.'

Barney still does not make eye contact when he takes it from me. 'Give me a minute. I can tell you exactly where this has last been.'

Charles thinks of us getting a coffee while we wait for Barney. Barney encourages us to go and he will come to us.

WHILE WE WALK over to the vending machine to get coffee, I ask Charles if he noticed Barney's odd behaviour but he does not give it a second thought. He puts it down to work overload and the fact that Barney does not like me. I sarcastically laugh at him and ask him again on a serious note. Charles still shrugs it off and puts it down to Barney having an off day.

I mention how he struggled to make eye contact with me and wonder if I have upset him somehow. Charles tells me that I am overthinking and it must be home life.

WHEN WE GET our coffee from the vending machine, I think about what happened in Shenzhen.

I broach the 'M' word; 'Do you remember what we talked about when we were caught in the moment?'

Charles behaves coolly and says, 'You'll have to remind me. We said quite a lot over those few days.'

I struggle not to blush. 'The last night we spent being intimate.'

Charles passes over my coffee from the vending machine as he recalls, 'Ah. The part when you said, "the way I make you smile". Right?'

I smack him against his arm, 'You know.'

Charles still mocks me, '"The way I make you be yourself"?'

I hit him again; 'Marry.'

Charles pretends to remember as he takes his coffee and slowly walks away, 'Oh. That. When you proposed to me.'

I walk after him and grab his suit blazer to pull him aside away from colleagues' prying eyes. Instead of having a talk, I find myself pushing myself on him and kissing him passionately. He responds and then smiles as he pulls away.

Charles stops playing around. 'When we get back from our assignment, we will look for a ring.'

I need to hear him say it again, 'What did you just say?'

Charles rolls his eyes, 'What is your preference for a diamond ring?'

I only care about getting engaged, so I say, 'I don't care. So long as it comes from you.'

We kiss again before returning to our desks.

WHILE WE WAIT for Barney to come to our desks, we resume what we were doing before Miles interrupted us. While I finish deleting old messages and Charles plays his card game, we cannot keep our eyes away from each other.

Barney seems to be taking longer than he usually takes to locate a last-known address. Finally, Barney comes over with information on Helen's last location.

BARNEY IS keen to tell us what he has found out. 'I took a little longer as you will not believe what I found out.'

I ask him to elaborate as I can see Charles is impatient; 'Can you get to the point?'

Barney waffles on, 'I went to find out her last location. When I did, I saw that it was on an island. I then went to find out what was on that island and I found out it belongs to a banker. His name is Epson Bernstein. It got me thinking. Why would a woman go missing from an island? Then I thought about finding the network supplier and then the name of the user.'

I hurry him along; 'Can you get to the end?'

Barney gets shirty; 'If you allow me to finish. I found out she is twelve. That got me to thinking why a twelve-year-old would be on an island with someone almost four times her age.'

Charles thinks out loud, 'The girl has no business being on an island with an adult who is not a relative.'

Barney smiles as the penny drops; 'So, I dug deeper. Raided the internet for everything on this Epson. It's not good. There have been tiny brushes with the law. Rumours without evidence.'

Charles makes an educated guess. 'The rumours tying him to under-age girls? Or at least questionable ethics with the opposite sex?'

I concur; 'Maybe her disappearance isn't random after all. Thanks, Barney.'

Charles has a hunch. 'Can you give us any known associates? Preferably over the phone. We need to pack for tomorrow.'

Barney is happy to find that out. 'I will give you the location of the island. You will need a boat to get out there. See you later.'

I almost completely forget about my appointment with my shrink at four o'clock, which is in the next ten minutes. We've been so hectic that time has gone by so quickly. I remind Charles and he is not fazed. He goes ahead with packing at home and will see me at his place. I concur and as I am about to go, Miles come up to us. I still leave so I do not miss my appointment.

Miles wants to know when we are leaving, 'You still here? I thought you were getting the next plane.'

Charles reminds him about the mobile enquiry; 'We asked Barney to locate the girl's mobile last use. Only found out now.'

Miles wants to know the location, 'Where?'

Charles mentions the area and adds, 'An island.'

Miles is baffled. 'I assume it is inhabited. Do you have a time?'

Charles says, 'He didn't tell us. We didn't ask. We will find out when we get there.'

Miles ponders, 'Where has Jane gone?

Charles is vague; 'Gone to an appointment.'

Miles wonders and then has a light bulb moment with a rhetorical response of knowing where she has gone.

I HAVE BEEN SEEING a psychotherapist over the past three and a half years since I began in October 2016. It became a requirement when joining The Agency.

The therapist's office is on another floor along a corridor with a glass railing. You can see down below to the ground floor and the other floors.

Before you get to his office door, there is a reception waiting area that is like a cave with a receptionist's desk on the right and a soft flat couch on the left.

I am virtually ready to stop therapy now except for my infrequent flashbacks. I will ask him about how to deal with my PTS when I finish my therapy.

While I am sat here waiting, with the lady receptionist smiling at me now and again, I think how great I feel. I have a great boyfriend, soon to be fiancé, and my past is not merged with my current and future life.

The thought of being at Charles' house in a couple of hours makes me excited. Somewhere to be after I leave here.

Before I know it, I hear the door open and see the person before me coming out. I do not know the person.

I wait for his voice to come through the intercom on the receptionist desk.

I GO INSIDE AND, as per usual, John is sat in his chair waiting for me to sit on a two-seater sofa opposite him.

I take my shoes off and cross my legs on his sofa. I watch him jotting down on his A4 pad of yellow paper while I make myself comfortable.

After a few minutes, he asks if I want a coffee or a cold drink. I tell him that I am coffeed out and okay for a drink.

John sits back into his recliner chair. 'So, how have you been since I last saw you? Give me a number from one to ten. One being completing depressed to ten being great. Now.'

I do not hesitate; 'Ten.'

John studies my posture. 'That is good. What is it that makes you feel that way?'

I immediately think of the last couple of days and say, 'I feel good. I have no hang-ups and I can think about my childhood past and my parents' death and not feel affected. I accept the past but I do not let it control my thoughts or feelings today. Ask me three years ago, I would have taken my life.'

John says some words that I thought I would say first, 'I think you are ready. I have given you the tools to deal with anything.'

I bring up my nightmares; 'I still get irregular dreams of my past conflicts. Especially when I was in Montenegro.'

John is confident that I will be fine, but to reassure me he says, 'I will make a CD for you. Play it as often as you like. If you feel you want to come here, my door is open.'

I relax about having my next nightmare. 'So, this is it?'

JOHN SMILES, 'Yes. The last four visits, you have come in consistently happy in your own skin. You have not got that weight on your shoulders.'

I feel like I am being released from jail. 'I don't know how to react. It is weird being told that I do not need to be here anymore.'

The rest of the time we talk about when I first came here. I had a broken arm from my first assignment and was very timid. I did not say a word in my first session. Now, it is more like two friends catching up. Before I leave, I have my last hypnotherapy in the chair and John gives me a CD to take with me.

## 9

# BACK IN

Charles and I go to my place to pack for The Virgin Islands. I live in London in zone two of Hackney. I cannot afford to buy my own place, so I rent a flat that overlooks Homerton Overground.

THE BLOCK of flats is in Sedgwick Street, off Homerton High Street. My rented apartment is inside a high-rise building with dark grey brickwork on the outside and white walls and white skirting boards inside the corridors and the apartments. The corridor floor is carpeted with ribbed dark grey carpet. There are glass balconies on alternate floors of the building. I am fortunate to have one of the balconies outside my rented apartment. The balcony wall is made of glass with a steel railing and with a concrete floor and matt cream plasterwork.

The flat is a one-bedroom apartment with a small separate kitchen that can only have one person in it at a time. There is also a separate living room that faces the train station. The balcony is off the living room.

The kitchen units are cream and brown with oblong metal handles. There is light brown Amtico flooring imitating a wooden floor.

The living room is a fair size; you could fit in a double bed with room on either side to walk around. I only have one sofa that seats two people and a flat-screen television placed on a wooden television stand in the corner, left of the balcony. I have a tall plant in a large circular blue ceramic plant bowl to the right of the balcony. I keep the living room in a minimalist layout because the room is small. I also have a small square dining table with four wooden seats near the back of the room in the corner, backing onto the kitchen wall.

My bedroom is a double room with a built-in wardrobe, which has mirrored glass on alternate doors. I have a side table on my preferred side of the bed with a bedside lamp. I sometimes like to read before going to sleep.

The bathroom is a six-foot-by-six-foot room with a bath and glass splash with a separate shower on the wall above the bath. The bath area is tiled from bath to ceiling. The tiles are rectangular and beige in colour. The floor is also Amtico, the same design as the kitchen.

The landlord chose the flooring when it was first being built. The landlord said at the time when I first moved in that I could change the colour of the walls, but I have kept all the walls inside the apartment in their original white with matt finish. The carpet throughout the whole apartment is beige, apart from the bathroom, which has a different flooring.

WHEN WE HAVE FINISHED PACKING, we think about having something to eat. We end up ordering a Chinese take away for delivery so we can relax and drink.

We are in my living room with a bottle of rosé open and I have my head in his lap on the sofa.

We talk about Helen going missing and wonder if she will be dead or hiding with a boyfriend. Charles wants to make sure we know how she died so we can give her father, Gordon, closure.

We wonder what it would be like with our kids and how disciplined we will be. The kids will wish they were never born.

Both of us end up laughing at the idea of two spies bringing up children. I almost spill my glass of wine as I struggle to control my laughter.

THE FOOD finally arrives and we sit at the table in comfortable silence while having our dinner. We begin to talk about buying a wedding ring and how soon we can go shopping. Practically, it will be when we get back from the Virgin Islands to report on the missing girl.

I mention children and how important they are to me. I ask for Charles' opinion and he can see a future with us having two children.

I ask him about working for The Agency after having children. I tell him that I see us no longer working there.

Charles agrees with our job not being sensible for raising children. He wants us to leave our employment for something with normal regular office hours.

It is nice to hear that we are on the same page and we have no preferences for a boy or girl.

I can imagine us living somewhere away from London, out in the country; somewhere like Milton Keynes.

The more the idea sinks in, the more I get excited about being engaged and planning for the future. This could mean being married around this time next year. I can see myself wearing a wedding dress for the first time and imagine how our kids will be.

I can see in Charles' eyes how he likes the idea of getting married and taking the kids to the park. He admits to me that he never thought he would be given a second chance to find love and have children.

The next morning, we are on our flight to Charlotte Amalie. To get to the island, we have to take a boat. We are going to verify the body first before finding out what happened on the island.

Charles is asleep while I stare out of the window at the horizon.

I cannot stop thinking about going shopping for wedding rings. I place my wedding hand against the back of the seat in front of me and imagine a diamond ring on my finger. I wonder what type of shape it will be.

I picture us going to Hatton Garden after work before the shops close, going into every shop and trying on every ring.


WE ARRIVE in Charlotte Amalie at two o'clock local time after half an hour's delay. Once we get out of the airport, we go to our hotel, the Windward Passage Hotel. It is less than ten minutes from Cyril E King International Airport.


WE ARRIVE at the hotel and go straight to our room. I still cannot stop thinking about having children and leaving this game.

Charles can tell that my mind is preoccupied but he leaves me to it. We are to go to the police to find out if they have any new information, then head to the island unannounced and question the person living there.

We both take a shower together with Charles discussing the assignment in regards to finding the officer in charge. I am listening but my mind is elsewhere. Normally, we would be intimate in the shower but this time, I am happy to just wash each other.

Once we are both dry and refreshed, we push past our jet lag to begin our investigation.


THE VIRGIN ISLANDS POLICE DEPARTMENT is only a seven-minute taxi ride away. We walk up some grey stone steps that are really clean. There are shrubs on either side leading up to the double doors of the police station.

The building appears modern and clean as if we are in Beverly Hills in America. The island itself feels clean and free of rubbish.

Inside, they have a big lobby with marble flooring and fresh clean matt finish

WE WALK into the lobby and it appears grand with sandy brown marble flooring. The reception area is quiet so we get seen straight away.

All the patrons are holiday-makers, with us being the only apparent business people. I feel out of place seeing guests in shorts, swimwear and casual summer clothes.

After we check in and have our luggage taken to our room, we go to one of the hotel's clothes shops for sensible attire.

The weather here is in the high twenties.

WHILE WE SOURCE OUR CLOTHES, we discuss the probability of the twelve-year-old girl being at the coroner's office. I express my opinion first and assume she will have a head injury as cause of death.

Charles makes his prediction as he shuffles through the short-sleeved shirts, 'I know the body will be there. I think it will be ruled as a misadventure. I think it will involve underage drinking.'

By the time we finish having our discussion, we have finished shopping for holiday clothes and pay at the till.

We eventually go to our hotel room and change out of our business clothes into more comfortable wear.

WE ARRIVE at the police station to find out where the coroner's office is. The lobby area floor is coated in sandy dust from outside.

The walls are orange with a faded blue and maroon checkered floor at a diagonal angle. The ceiling is white and the area is aged.

It seems like a ghost town and you would expect a tumbleweed to roll along the floor. It does not even appear that anyone is here.

CHARLES TAPS on a dull brass bell to have someone come and speak to us. It takes a couple of minutes for a police officer to see us.

A desk clerk finally comes through a door and we catch a glimpse of an open office in the back. The clerk is a tall, slim, black man and appears to be in his late twenties.

I ask if he can tell us where their coroner's office is and if he is aware of a Jane Doe body. The man is not in a position to hear any rumours.

However, he is able to point us in the right direction where we will find out.

He directs us to go back outside and walk round towards the back and we will see a separate building on the back of the police station.


WHILE WE TAKE our time walking round the back, Charles asks me how I would feel if we found an engagement ring during our stay here. I like the idea but feel weird trying to enjoy buying a ring while finding a missing Helen. Charles rethinks his idea and agrees with me and is happy to wait till we return home.

Out of the blue, Charles asks me to move in with him permanently. It surprises me as we have been together for four years and have never considered it. Our work takes us away for days at a time and so we do not have time to discuss these things.

I think to ask him about our future, 'Where do you see us living in five years' time?'

Charles opens the double glass doors for us as we walk into the coroners building. 'I don't want our kids growing up in London. I would rather live out in the suburbs. Travel by train into London. If we find jobs still in the city.'

I am surprised to hear him say that; 'That is what I was thinking.'

We reach a glass wall with a glass door where we see a tall man in his white scrubs.


INSIDE THE BUILDING is a wide corridor that has dark brown marble walls and a dark grey concrete floor. A row of skylights creates natural light in the passageway.

There are four mortuary examining rooms with domed glass walls and a glass door. Each room has a mortuary cabinet with four rows of five chambers.

Only one of the four examination rooms has its lights on and there is only one man there. He is Caucasian with thin short straight dark grey hair. He is six feet tall with a thin frame and slightly arched over. He is clean-shaven with an oval head. He is in his fifties and has pale skin.


THE MAN NOTICES us and comes to the door to ask if we are lost or looking for someone. We explain who we are and show our identification. We tell him that we are wondering if he has had a Jane Doe come in over the past week.

The man remembers a young girl coming through and we tell him that it is likely to relate to our enquiry. He walks us into his room and takes us over to the morgue cabinet.

We watch him pull open one of the cabinet doors and pull out a stretcher at chest level. He then pulls back the sheet covering her body. I take out my phone with a picture of Helen's face and make a comparison. We are sad to see that it is the twelve-year-old girl, Helen.

We ask him what he has discovered about her body. He is brief and mentions four observations. He takes us through the various findings.

He tells us that he found a leaf, sand under her nails, water in her mouth and a white substance inside her nasal passage. Also, shrimps, not fully digested, olives, tomato, cheese and alcohol in her stomach.

We ask if he has the results of the white powder and anything on the leaf. The man explains that he gave the samples to forensics to be tested. Charles asks if we can have a copy of the forensic report. The man tells us that we can get a hold of the report from his computer.

As he tells us that, a man walks in casually and it appears that the coroner knows him.

WE ARE INTERRUPTED by a Caucasian man who is a little taller than me, with a slightly protruding belly, dressed in a light grey two-piece suit. His brown tie is loose around his neck and he appears dishevelled. He has a filled-out face with a well-groomed thin black beard. His hair is thick, wavy and brushed back. He appears to be in his late forties.

He has come to speak to the coroner. 'Hi, Mortimer.'

Mortimer corrects him; 'Dr Mortimer, Detective Monroe.'

Detective Monroe smiles. 'Excuse me. And who are these two?'

I lead the conversation; 'My name is Jane Knight and his name is Charles May. We work for our government and were sent here to look into the disappearance of a politician's daughter.'

Detective Monroe briefly holds our attention before talking to the examiner. 'I have the results of the white powder and leaf. The sand and sea water are too common to distinguish.'

The examiner is curious and asks for the results. 'What does the report say?'

Detective Monroe summarises the information; 'She had taken cocaine and the leaf is rare and found in only half a dozen places.'

Charles is curious about the leaf. 'How rare are you talking?'

Detective Monroe checks the folder again. 'It cannot be found on this island. Does that help?'

I have a question - 'How was her body discovered?'

Detective Monroe answers, 'A couple were going for a stroll on the promenade when they spotted the body by some rocks on the beach.'

I ask for the Doctor's opinion; 'Do you know how she died?'

Dr Mortimer has a theory. 'Cocaine and alcohol intake? I suggest the cocktail made her have an overdose. Accidental death. There is no bruising, no wounds. So, misadventure stroke accident.'

I think about assistance. 'Could she have had alcohol plied on her without her consent, even with the cocaine?'

Dr Mortimer does not ponder on the question. 'There is no way of telling. But if you want an indication, her lungs would be filled with alcohol. Her lungs were not filled, which means she died before there was any chance of drowning in alcoholic liquid.'

Charles makes a statement; 'She died somewhere else and her body was dumped here. She had a staple diet of shrimp, olives, tomato, cheese and caviar. I don't think she would have found a caviar eatery place near the beach before dying. So, where did she manage to have caviar?'

Detective Monroe is surprised by how meticulous we are. 'Who are you guys?'

Charles answers for both of us, 'We work for the British government. We are paid to be suspicious.'

Detective Monroe smiles. 'A double o seven.'

Charles almost laughs; 'Something like that. But without the gadgets.'

Detective Monroe chortles, 'Yeah. That was funny. Do you have a license to kill?'

I respond to his question, 'No. But we have diplomatic immunity.'

Detective Monroe is speechless and nothing more is discussed.

Our next point of call is the island. Find the owner and interrogate him. I know Charles is thinking the same.

We thank Dr Mortimer for his time explaining to us what he found and giving his professional opinion.

Before we leave, I take a photo of the girl's face as evidence for Miles' friend Gordon Wrex. I plan on forwarding the photo to Miles for him to break the sad news. We know that Miles will want to know who is to blame, so, finding the person responsible for her death will give the parents closure.

Once we find that person, we can go home and do our real job.

Dr Mortimer gets our attention as we go to leave. 'There is one more thing that I noticed. I only found one earring on her. Maybe the other one could still be at the place where she died.'

We stare at each other and thank Dr Mortimer for his time.


DETECTIVE MONROE quickly finishes up with the coroner and hurries to catch up with us. He walks us out of the building and follows up on our last conversation.

He asks what we do and why two agents are interested in a non-profile child. We tell him that it is a request by our people and not our forte.

He stops us in our tracks by the steps to the front of the police station. Detective Monroe wants to know what our next move is. We are not keen to divulge our plans in detail as we do not want any interference by him or anyone else. But Charles feels oblige to hint that we know where the rare leaf is from. Detective Monroe is intrigued and asks us where. Charles and I glance at each other and then tell him; Epson Bernstein's place.

Detective Monroe ponders on our theory and is quick to go off and do something.

# 10

# UPDATE

When we get back to the hotel, I lie on our bed and Charles walks over to the desk and rests himself against it.

Charles wants to phone Miles to let him know what we have found out so far. He taps his mobile on his chin as he ponders how he will tell him. I explain that there is no easy way but to tell the truth. Charles sighs loudly.

Charles goes to make the call to Miles but has reservations as he pauses before pushing the dial button. I lie across the bed on my side, facing him, as I wait for him to call.

I ask him to put his mobile on loudspeaker so I can hear the phone ring from Miles' end before he answers. We hear the long dial tone for a few seconds before he picks up.

Miles eventually responds and asks Charles if we have made any headway in our investigation.

Charles pauses briefly, then says, 'We found Helen. Unfortunately, it is not good news. We discovered that she is dead. We saw Helen's body in the morgue.'

Miles goes quiet for a while, then he says, 'So, do we know how she died?'

Charles recounts what the coroner mentioned. 'She died by misadventure, drinking alcohol and taking cocaine. Some passers-by noticed her on the beach. It was staged.'

Miles wants to know more answers. 'How did Helen get hold of alcohol and drugs?'

Charles uses our theory. 'We believe she was on an island and some people there supplied the alcohol and drugs.'

Miles wants to know what our next move is. 'Are you satisfied with the answers? Will you be coming back now?'

Charles explains what our next move is; 'Before we came here, we got Barney to give us the last-known position of Helen's mobile. It was on an island that we believe she died on. We plan on going to the island tomorrow to find out who caused her to overdose.'

Miles is happy with our progress. 'Once you are finished there, come home. We need you to start on a new assignment.'

Charles agrees with him. 'We will be home in two days.'

Miles is thankful and says, 'I appreciate all your effort. It is why I asked you two to go. Say thanks to Jane.'

I hear the conversation. 'No worries. See you in a couple of days.'

Miles thinks out loud; 'I will tell Gordon what we know so far and confidently tell him that we will find her murderer.'


AFTER WE FINISH SPEAKING to Miles, I ask Charles what he wants to do now. He suggests going out for dinner somewhere within walking distance.

We have a shower and change into evening wear. Charles changes into a shirt and trousers while I put on a dress.


WE FIND a nice French restaurant by the sea with the moonlight shimmering across the water. We take a table by the window overlooking the ocean. While we wait for our order to arrive, we talk about our final day tomorrow.

Charles says, 'We will charter a boat to take us to the island. We make it clear that we know she died there. We ask the owner what happened so we can conclude how why she died.'

I agree with him. 'It will not take long to find out what happened. We might as well organise our flight for tomorrow. It won't take all day to get an answer. This is a closure exercise.'

Charles changes the subject; 'I like the dress you're wearing. It brings out your eyes.'

I roll my eyes and begin to think about our time in Shenzhen. 'I cannot believe you inadvertently proposed on our last assignment.'

Charles smiles and I can see what he is remembering. 'You proposed to me. And it is not even a leap year.'

I do not remember it like that. 'I could read your mind and I was only saying what you were thinking.'

Charles laughs at me, 'Right. You were hoping that I was thinking it and making an assumption.'

I laugh sarcastically and say, 'You owe me a ring. I will even give you the money for it.'

Charles stops laughing and gazes at me. 'You are still as beautiful as when I first met you. We can look for a ring here. Buy one tomorrow.'

I really want that but I see us window shopping in London. 'I really want to find a ring too. But I want to wait till we get home. I think it will be more fun.'

Charles understands, 'Then we buy a ring as soon as we get back to London.'

I think about us having children, so I add, 'I suddenly thought about having kids. I wonder how we would react if we found out it was our child.'

Charles knows how he would feel. 'I would connect their balls to the mains and cook them.'

I admire him even more. 'How many kids do you see us having?'

Charles gives an answer without a thought; 'Three. How many would you like?'

I have to think about it, then reply, 'I want two.'

Charles is curious, 'How soon would you like children?'

'I would like to have kids within the next couple of years.'

Charles is on the same page as me. 'The next question is how do we juggle family life and work-life? It is not exactly nine to five and our job is not exactly stable and normal.'

I have already decided what we need to do if ever had kids. 'I would definitely give up my job. When the time comes for going back to work, I would go back to working for an accountancy firm. I would like you to change your job.'

Charles wonders what he could do for another career. 'I don't know how my resumé will get me a change of career.'

I come up with a few ideas; 'You could be a fireman or a security guard.'

Charles does not see himself as doing either of those roles. 'I think consulting, or a bodyguard for an unimportant person who lives in the UK.'

I like the sound of that. 'Whatever you decide to do, as long as it is in England and doesn't involve shooting and avoiding bombs.'

Our meal arrives so we finish our conversation and enjoy our dinner.


ON OUR WAY back to the hotel, I cannot help staring at Charles through a different pair of eyes. I feel the urge to make love when we get back to the hotel.

.  .  .

WHEN WE GET BACK to our room, we both have the same idea and have a shower first before going to bed.

Charles is first into the double shower cubicle and I follow him soon after. I walk in with a towel wrapped round me.

I take my time peeling off the towel to reveal my breasts in front of Charles.

I notice him admiring my mounds like he has never seen them before and gazes at my bum when I turn round to hang the towel over the shower glass.

I crave his affection as I study his torso and cannot help pouncing on him. I sense that he has been missing this as well.

We hug each other under the showerhead and passionately kiss. As we have not had any sexual activity, I can feel his erection pressing against my stomach which reassures me that we still have chemistry.

I caress his manhood with my fingertips, stroking it up and down to get him more aroused. This makes him press harder against my body. I squeeze his shaft occasionally in the palm of my hand.

We heavily peck at each other's mouths under the showerhead and I put my arms around him. He moves me against the wall while the water streams down our bodies. He parts my legs and then lifts me up with my legs in his arms.

I then feel him slide inside me and enjoy the feeling of him sliding in and out of me. We have not made love in the shower before. I can feel him stretching when he enters inside me each time.

I feel my bum being gently smacked against the wall with each thrust he makes inside me. I do not want him to cum yet as I want to continue in bed.

Charles quietly tells me that he wants to get out of the shower and continue on the bed. We finish cleaning ourselves and then get dry. I motion Charles to sit on the end of the bed, naked, and lie on his back.

I then kneel between his legs and run my tongue slowly along his length. I like the scent from the soap on his skin as I taste him. I hear his signals to know that I am arousing him and enjoy making him satisfied.

I place him in my mouth and gently suck his end as I feel him getting hard again. Once I get him to stand to attention, I slide my tongue up and down his vertical shaft. I also make eye contact with Charles as I swirl my tongue around his end.

I feel him twitch and know that he is about to cum like a fountain as he has done in the past. I can hear him straining as he is feeling himself about to ejaculate.

I see clear liquid pour out before he actually cums. I avoid getting myself covered as I pull away and watch him create a volcano.

His body stiffens and jolts like electricity is running through him. I smile as I watch him enjoying the feeling.

He sits up and leans forward for a kiss. I smile as we peck on the lips before going in for a full deep kiss. I stop smiling as we lose ourselves.

Charles changes places with me and he wants to give me oral.


I FEEL him working on my clitoris which relaxes me and I enjoy the feeling. I can see myself falling asleep as I get lethargic.

I slowly feel myself getting aroused and instinctively widen my legs to encourage him to keep going. It is not long before I feel him using a finger inside me, while he continues working on my clitoris. I begin to groan as I enjoy how he always gets me going. It is not long before I feel myself getting wetter and my breathing sounds deeper.

Charles listens to my signs and picks up speed as he hears me making shorter breaths. Eventually, my body shudders and I give a final loud groan as I cum. He continues to work his fingers inside me to make me have multiple orgasms.

When he knows that I have no more orgasm to give, he subsides and then lies next to me and we cuddle.


AFTER I RECOVER from my oral, we make love on top of the bedsheets. I manage to cum again but Charles finds that I am too wet to be able to have another orgasm. Eventually, we finish and fall asleep.


## A Way In


THE NEXT MORNING, we search for businesses that provide boat hire. There are a few to choose from and we find an available fishing boat in Cay Bay. We have to be there for eleven o'clock to fill out the paperwork and take the boat out.

We think it will be a two-hour boat ride to reach the island. Our stay should only be about an hour and then we will head back here to check out of our room and head home.

Once we finish making our plans, we get ready for the day. We wear fresh clothes, similar to yesterday.

We cannot keep our eyes off each other after last night. I cannot wait till we get back so we can buy my engagement ring and begin planning our wedding. I can see us getting married this time next year, then starting our family a year later.

When we are both ready, we go downstairs for breakfast.


DURING BREAKFAST, Charles and I check what we need to take with us besides our guns and mobiles. Then, we pack what we do not take with us in our luggage. We decide to pay for our room before we leave and have our luggage kept in their baggage storeroom.

While we discuss what to take with us, we see Detective Monroe walking over to the reception desk. Charles stands up and waves for his attention. The detective notices us as approaches reception and excuses himself to the person behind the check-in desk.

He walks over towards us, smiling and acknowledging Charles. I move one of our chairs to allow him to sit down and motion for tea or coffee.


DETECTIVE MONROE APPEARS chirpy like he has some excellent news. We are curious about what he has to tell us.

We both stand up out of courtesy to welcome him and wait for him to take a seat. Charles pours out a cup of coffee after Detective Monroe chooses his preference. After we are all sat down, we wait for him to tell us his news.

Detective Monroe takes a sip of his coffee, then says, 'I thought about what you said yesterday. So, I spoke to the courts and had them write me out a warrant. I thought you guys may want to tag along.'

Charles is happy to hear that and asks, 'When will you go to the island?'

Detective Monroe is keen; 'Today. I hear he has a cocktail party for some potential investors. I hear he is leaving for America tomorrow and so our only opportunity is today. Are you two up for getting a boat to the island?'

I think today is getting better and better. 'We happened to book a boat for eleven o'clock to head out there. Fancy tagging along with us?'

Detective Monroe smiles and sips his coffee in glee; 'Of course. Shall I meet you there or wait here?'

Charles answers his question, 'If you have a car here, you can wait for us and drive us to the marina.'

Detective Monroe is happy to drive us, so he asks, 'Where should I wait for you?'

Charles thinks briefly, 'We will meet you outside the front entrance. We should only be ten minutes.'

Detective Monroe finishes his coffee. 'See you outside.'

. . .

CHARLES and I are glad that the detective is coming with us as he can ask the questions. We can also use him to distract Epson while we explore his island to see where Helen may have died.

While we pack our last things in our travel bags, we end up also taking our work credit cards to pay for the charter. I make one more sweep of the hotel room to make sure we have not left anything behind.


CHARLES PAYS the bill while I check our luggage into storage. Once Charles finishes paying, we go to find the detective outside.


DETECTIVE MONROE DRIVES a Cadillac Sudan which is a saloon in the UK. He is very talkative about himself and his family. He has two boys in their teens and his wife works as a teacher. Charles is in direct earshot as he is sat in the front.

Luckily, it only takes five minutes to reach the boat hire business.


THE SALES OFFICE is along a promenade of shops and eateries overlooking the harbour. There are two people wearing shorts and labelled polo shirts advertising the business.

The detective stands around outside while we fill in their forms and pay a deposit as well as the fee to hire the boat for the day.

We get the key to the boat and then the three of us walk to the pontoon opposite the shop.


THE FISHING BOAT is thirty feet long and white with a chrome railing at the front. It comes with fishing rods even though we are not going to catch any fish.

As we leave the harbour, we struggle to find any marine charts inside the cabin. So, we find an app on one of our mobiles to download a chart of the local sea in our area.

We travel at a comfortable speed of sixty-five knots and our estimated time of arrival is an hour and a half; less than I thought it would take.


THE GUESTS ATTENDING the island for afternoon cocktails and a short presentation of a new investment are provided with transportation.

Epson has supplied a two-tier charter boat for twenty visitors to be able to drink and enjoy canapés. There is champagne being served by waiters on the boat during the journey. It allows the passengers to break the ice between themselves before they arrive on the island.

The guests are a mixture of businessmen and women and trust funds with people who already know Epson. It also includes a judge who has been involved in hiding Epson's child-trafficking activity.

They are dressed in smart but casual evening wear.

They left Charlotte Amalie half an hour before Jane and Charles.


ONE OF THE guests is a black African/American woman with flawless mahogany skin, in her late thirties. She has a cool afro hairstyle shaped into a four-inch-high quiff with a grade zero strip that goes around the base of her neck and behind her ears. The back and sides of her hair are cut at a grade six.

She has high cheekbones and an oblong face with a slim nose.

Her height is six foot seven, with long shapely legs and an athletic build.

She is wearing a fitted white dress that falls down to her ankles and has a long slit along her left leg. The dress has thin shoulder straps.

Her home is in Los Angeles, where she works for a corporation that acts like The Agency but is called D.I.A.M.O.N.D.S. They are a low-key intelligence organisation that operates under the radar.

Her name is Stellar Star.


SHE IS on a mission to follow a man who her organisation has been searching for. They have a lead to a man who crossed paths with him. Hence the reason why she has made herself available on the guest list to interrogate Epson.

Stellar socialises with the other guests to blend in and appear part of the group.


EVENTUALLY, the charter boat arrives at Epson's island and docks at the pontoon. Two waiters are standing in front of the house with a tray each of sparkling wine for their arrival.

When each invitee has a glass, the waiters walk them round the side of the house along the sandstone path with shrubs on either side. The walkway splits into two - to the right behind the house to a small patio, or to the left to a larger patio. The waiters go left towards the bigger patio. It is shaped like a sea shell and overlooks the ocean. There is a black railing that goes all the way round.

There are additional waiters already waiting on the patio carrying trays of canapés. A couple of young female violinists are providing gentle music.

The guests continue conversing amongst each other and occasionally laugh.

Stellar gives subtle smiles as she walks among them and, at the same time, is patiently waiting for Epson's appearance. She wants to pull him to one side and question him about her target and find out where she can find him.

Epson is inside his house waiting for his guests to settle in before making an appearance.

WE ARE NOT FAR NOW as we can see the island in the distance. The mobile app tells us that we are five minutes away.

During our journey, we have learnt about the detective's whole life. We have also briefly told him what we do for a living and who we work for.

Detective Monroe pestered us on how we were confident that Helen's last-known location was on the island. We eventually told him that we had her last mobile signal and that the triangulation pin-pointed Epson's doorstep.

I suggest we should check our guns for ammunition and make sure they are ready to use. We organise what Charles and I will do while Detective Monroe is interviewing about the death.

As soon as we reach the island, we notice that there are a couple of speedboats and a charter boat moored up. So, we assume that this is where we dock ourselves.

Once the fishing boat is tied up, we walk onto the pontoon and head towards the house.

IT APPEARS quiet but we can hear indistinct chatter and follow the sound to see if Epson is there. After we walk up the side of the house and bear left, we soon discover a party.

Epson appears and we hear him announce his presence to his guests. 'Welcome to my island. I hope you are enjoying free drinks and food.'

People quietly laugh at his comment but we do not show any amusement.

Epson continues, 'You have been invited to have an opportunity to invest in a new project that is already taking the market by storm. But we are at the cusp of the waves. I am asking you to invest half a million dollars each. Tonight is a way of showing my appreciation of your investment.'

Once Epson finishes talking, Detective Monroe approaches him and asks to speak to him in private.

Charles and I see this opportunity to slope off and check out the beach for any evidence of where Helen died.

WHILE WE WALK along a path that is parallel to the beach, I make a point of staring at the ground on either side of the footpath. I try to find any type of loose fibre, hair or the earring to get an indication of where she walked.

It is not long before something catches my eye; a glint of a turquoise-coloured object that gives me a flashback to what the coroner showed us. I get Charles' attention and crouch down to take a closer view.

My heart sinks as it becomes more of a realisation that she died here. It is the missing earring that matches her other one. I almost get emotional as I imagine her being one of my nieces. Charles places his hand on my shoulder to give me comfort. We have the location where she died.

Charles behaves like it is one of my sibling's children. 'It is okay, Jane. Come on. Let's find Epson and get her father some closure.'

I glance at Charles and gesture in agreement. 'I want to make him suffer. For all the girls.'

Charles gives me a stern gaze; 'Absolutely.'

We go back towards the house to find Detective Monroe with Epson.

EPSON HAS TAKEN Detective Monroe inside his house to his study room on the ground floor. He is sat behind his glass desk and Detective Monroe is seated in front of his desk.

Epson only responds to questions rather than opening himself up to prosecution. He is curious to know how the detective linked the girl to his island. Epson is eager to know how he connected the dots together without giving away his involvement.

He responds to Monroe's questions with vague responses and not really giving straight answers.

Detective Monroe is used to slippery customers and so he keeps his cool and uses different angles to try to trip him up.

Epson pauses, then says, 'I really wish I could help you. What makes you think she was at one of my parties?'

Detective Monroe smiles sarcastically. 'Of course. She had a mobile and do you know where it last pinged?'

Epson appears off guard. 'So, where did you last see her mobile?'

Detective Monroe gloats, 'Here on this island. How do you explain that?'

Epson thinks on his feet. 'Must have been a gate-crasher. We get those all the time.'

Detective Monroe knows that he has him; 'What kind of parties do you host?'

Epson has a puzzled expression, 'I'm not sure what you are implying.'

Detective Monroe senses that he will fold, so he continues, 'She was found with cocaine as well as alcohol in her system. She was only twelve. How did drugs get on your island?'

Epson does not show any concern as he answers, 'I cannot help that my guests want to bring excitement to my island. I personally do not take drugs. Let me see what I think happened. She was told about one of my parties. She asked to be invited, then got herself involved with people taking drugs. Hardly my fault.'

Detective Monroe finds he has an answer for everything. 'I can have you arrested for allowing narcotics to be used on your premises.'

Epson seems to think that he is untouchable. 'Do I need to get a lawyer?'

Detective Monroe is about to say something when Jane and Charles walk through the door.


WE SEE Epson with a confident composure and Detective Monroe's face shows he is not getting anywhere.

Epson is perplexed when he sees us walk in and demands, 'Who are you?'

Charles does not like how Epson has a smug face through not being tied to Helen's death. 'The name's May, Charles May.'

I introduce myself separately; 'Knight, Jane Knight. Have you managed to get the answers we need, Detective Monroe?'

Detective Monroe is showing a dislike for Epson. 'I am working on it.'

Epson is getting disgruntled with two more people giving him hassle. 'I should have you thrown off my island.'

Charles blanks his comment and grabs the back of his chair then pulls him round to the front of his desk. Epson is too stunned to react and wonders what he is going to do.

Charles shows anger in his eyes as he threatens, 'I see the normal questioning is not working. Let's try my way. You don't have to be here, Monroe.'

Detective Monroe does not know whether to stay or not be involved. 'Is it legal?'

I explain what our methods are. 'We do anything to prise out information. We don't work within your perimeter of the law. If you feel uncomfortable watching how we do things, I suggest you wait outside.'

Detective Monroe thinks for a second, then says, 'I'll stay to see the arrogance wiped off his face.'

I smile as I am glad that he is staying. 'See how we extract information.'

Epson is now worried for the first time and says, 'You can't make me do anything. The detective can even tell you.'

Detective Monroe replies to the contrary; 'I gave you a chance to confess to me. I guess you will have to confess the hard way. They have jurisdiction over me.'

I watch Epson panic as Charles grabs his lamp from the desk and rips the shade off. Charles then smashes the light bulb on the corner of the glass desk, leaving the live filament exposed.

Charles explains what he is going to do; 'Now, I am going to ask a bunch of questions. Each time you don't give a straight answer, I will light your balls. Which part of that sentence did you not understand?!'

I try not to smirk when I see Epson's face turn to terror, then I reinforce the action by saying, 'Trust me. You don't want to see him when he gets angry.'

Epson is quick to be submissive; 'Wait! Just wait. What is it you want to know?'

I turn to Detective Monroe. 'What are you waiting for? Ask away.'

Detective Monroe gathers his thoughts, then says, 'Right. Where was I? Ah, yes. We found her mobile's last-known location here. Did you kill her?'

Epson still hesitates; 'What does it matter? It was just a girl.'

Charles shoves the end of the lamp into his groin and a surge of electricity flows through his genitals.

Detective Monroe cannot quite believe what he is seeing. 'I think he is ready to talk. I don't think he is going to give us any more bull.'

Epson recovers from the pain with his voice distorted, 'Okay, one of my guests allowed her to take the drugs. She overdosed.'

Detective Monroe has one last question; 'How did she end up on Charlotte Amalie?'

Epson is quick to tell us, 'I had my men take her off the island and make it look like she died there.'

Charles has other questions; 'Are you trafficking children here?'

Epson hesitates and I watch Charles shove the lamp into his groin again. He squeals like a baby and is no longer self-confident.

Epson catches his breath; 'Okay. Okay. Yes.'

I ask a question, 'How long have you been trafficking?'

Epson instantly blurts out the answer, 'Ten years!'

Charles feels that it warrants another quick zap and shoves the lamp into his privates again. Detective Monroe feels out of his depth as he worries, 'That can't be good. His voice has gone funny.'

Charles scowls at the detective. 'He has been trafficking girls barely close to puberty.'

Detective Monroe thinks for a second then adds, 'You have a point. Let me have a go.'

Epson shouts out, 'What else do you want to know?'

I see Charles going to electrify him again, so I shout, 'Wait! Is there anything else that we should know?'

Epson shows a sign of relief when Charles stops. 'I know who you are!'

I touch Charles' arm and motion him to step away. 'You know who?'

Epson stares directly at me. 'I know who you are, Jane Knight.'

## 11

## A NAME FROM THE PAST

Stellar has been wondering how long Epson has been with a man wearing a grey two-piece suit. She remembers him having a groomed thin black beard. After quickly finishing her drink and placing the glass flute on the tray of the next waiter passing by, she goes to find him.

THERE IS a helicopter inbound that was sent in by The Order after one of the staff eavesdropped on the conversation. He contacted Lucas and he informed The Order.

The helicopter is carrying a Gatling gun that can tear through flesh like paper. It is a few minutes away and they plan on keeping Epson quiet permanently.

CHARLES, Detective Monroe and I glance at each other in surprise. Detective Monroe shrugs off his involvement.

I have no idea how he recognizes me, 'How do you know who I am?'

Epson is still dealing with the pain as he fidgets in the chair; 'Perhaps you are more familiar with The Order.'

I wonder if he recognizes my partner, 'What about Charles?'

Epson does not recognise him. 'I have never heard of him.'

Charles wants to know more; 'Talk.'

Epson explains, 'About three years ago, my client approached me to discuss a new type of investment. I thought it was strange considering it did not involve The Order's finances. They gave me another contact to create a new portfolio. They gave me your details to allow me to take a loan out in your name.'

I cannot believe what I am hearing. 'But that is impossible. I have never given my details to anyone. Who did you go to?'

Epson takes a breather then answers, 'Ivor Peteski. I was told that he would get what I needed to set up an investment plan.'

My jaw drops and I stare at Charles. 'But why would Ivor do that to me? We are friends.'

Epson does not care about my question. 'I just do what my clients ask for.'

Charles thinks out loud, 'Montenegro. Your wallet. It went missing briefly and ended up at reception.'

I have flashbacks to that fight I had which almost killed me. 'I remember. Everything falls into place. Ivor took my wallet. He must have taken it during my fight with Vladimir's sister.'

Charles agrees, 'But nothing was taken out of your wallet.'

I think back to that day. 'I questioned why my contents were shuffled with nothing missing.'

Epson sees me ponder and rolls his eyes and sarcastically fills in the blanks; 'He made copies of your contents. How on earth does your body function without a brain? I can see why he finds you annoying.'

I am confused now. 'Who finds me annoying?'

Epson gives me a name, 'Xavier.'

Charles thinks back three years ago. 'Ivor mentioned him in Montenegro. If he is liaising directly with you, then he must be the head of The Order. Logically, from the work we do, officers of any company will get involved in financial investments. Not some assistant. What does he look like?'

Epson gives a description, 'He has grey hair and is bald on top. He has a full black beard. He is about six foot tall and slim.'

His description rings a bell with me. 'We saw him that time in the Cayman Islands. At that meeting where we saw Vladimir.'

Charles ponders as he puts his hand to his chin. 'So, we must be getting close to them without us knowing. But how? What kind of investment did you make for Jane and how?'

Epson tells us, 'I used a loan in her name from the things she had in her wallet and invested the money in the black market, leaving three years' worth of audit trail.'

I use my accounting head, 'To tie me to illegal trade, it would have to be something substantial and believable. How much loan did you take out? And how did you manage to do that when I don't have a great financial credit score as I don't have loans or a mortgage?'

Epson answers my questions. 'With The Order's contacts and

resources, it is not exactly hard to find out someone's financial background. You came into inheritance money. The total value of £262,500 in cash and equity. It was easy to take out a loan and use your assets as collateral. It was luck that you did not liquidate your assets before taking the loan out.'

Charles is shocked. 'You took a secure loan out for £262,500?'

Epson gestures like it is loose change. 'Now you know that The Order will use the three years of transactions of buying and selling on the dark web in case you become too much of a threat.'

I think laterally with my fountain of knowledge of ways to launder money. 'If you have been trading in the deep dark web, you would need an account that cannot be traced by the taxman. Like a crypto account. And would have to have a bank account where it is held. This is why The Order has managed to stay under the radar. We wouldn't have known as they have companies which we assumed funded their activities. This is bigger than we first thought.'

Charles can see that I have a theory. 'What are you thinking?'

I make an assumption, 'Whatever they are up to, they needed more than just trading income to fund their projects. And the amount needed to accumulate that kind of money, SEC would have been triggered to investigate. What better way not to be detected by trading on a non-regulated market like crypto? Tell me I am wrong.'

Epson concurs with me, 'I trade their money in various cryptocurrencies such as Bitcoins, Ripple Litecoin, Ethereum coins and NEO coins. You can buy whatever you want using the cryptocurrencies.'

Charles has a thought; 'Where do they keep the financial records of these crypto transactions?'

Epson gives us a tutorial; 'I use a peer-to-peer system that only exists electronically. This is held on network computers that are backed onto a blockchain. A blockchain is a virtual ledger that acts in the same way as book-keeping software.'

I interpret what he has said. 'The blockchain records all financial transactions including assets bought and sold. Where do you keep the blockchains - on this island? Or at your office in New York?'

Epson chortles, 'Not that easy. Blockchains are not like your iCloud book-keeping. You will have to fly to Switzerland, to Dundel, if you want to see the transactions.'

Charles wants to know more about the location. 'What does the place look like?'

Epson has never been there so he admits, 'All I know is that anyone can walk in. No money is held there and the servers are secure. You just need a password to access the account. And by the way you are looking at me, you want that.'

. . .

STELLAR IS STRUGGLING to find Epson while walking around the island and eventually asks one of the waiters. She uses the Epson investment idea as a reason to find him. The waiter tells her that he went inside with a man. She thanks him and decides to go in and if she is asked what she is doing, she will use the bathroom as an excuse.

As she goes to walk towards the pontoon to go in from the front, she hears a helicopter screaming overhead. She cannot see where it is flying as the size of the house is obscuring her view.

She runs to the front of the house to see if she can have a better angle to see whose helicopter it is. As she is trying to see who it is, she glimpses a piece of grey metal and then hears a unique noise.

Stellar bolts towards the house, preparing to smash the door open.


WE HAVE HEARD enough and are waiting for Epson to search for the password. He walks over to an inexpensive painting of a vase with a single daisy. He pulls the picture away from the wall and we realise it is hiding a safe.


THE MAN with the Gatling gun in the back of the helicopter begins firing at the exterior wall of Epson's study.


AS CHARLES and I stand near Detective Monroe, still seated, we hear a loud distinctive sound of bullets being fired. Charles grabs the detective and drags him down to the floor and I drop to the ground at the same time.

Epson is unlucky and takes the full force of the hail of machine-gun fire. The bullets go through him and into the wall. He dies instantly.

The power of the machine gun does not take long to leave crater holes in the wall, disintegrating the brickwork.

A black woman crashes through the door and dives to the ground. She then reaches up inside her slit skirt. I notice Charles gawping at her and I have to close his mouth as I see his jaw drop.

She takes out a small silver Jennings J-22 pistol and begins firing at the pilot.

After a few shots, she hits the windscreen causing the pilot to pull away.

Charles orders Detective Monroe to see that the guests are safe and make sure they leave the island safely. We do not find time to introduce ourselves to the lady as we run out of the demolished study room and out the back door of the house.

DETECTIVE MONROE HEADS to the patio while we run towards the sound of the helicopter. The noise directs us towards the pontoon as we run along the footpath.

We do not see where the black woman has gone as we head towards the sea.

The helicopter makes a fly-by and begins firing at us and we instinctively dive into the water off the pontoon. We wait for a few seconds before submerging. We cannot see where they went. We see speedboats and swim towards them. We know that they will be faster than our fishing boat. Also, Detective Monroe will need to find his own way back.

## 12

## UNDER FIRE

We clamber onto one of the speedboats from the water. I climb on first with Charles helping by pushing me up. I then hold my arm out for him to grab hold of me and I help him on board.

Charles gets behind the wheel and starts the engine straight away. We zoom off as the helicopter fires at us again.

WE POWER underneath the helicopter and watch it turn around to chase us. Charles was hoping to follow it to see where they would be heading, but we are being pursued instead. Charles begins to open up the engine and pick up speed to try and outrun the pilot.

There is no let-up of the constant attack while we try to create a distance between us. I feel helpless not being able to return fire or help Charles out.

For some reason, I feel the need to check that we have enough fuel to get us back to the main island as well as dodging gunfire. We have over a tank full and so we will have enough to make it back.

We get the full brunt of the speedboat crashing through the ocean as we cruise at full speed. My hair is beginning to loosen with the rush of wind taking control.

I'm annoyed that we left our guns back at the hotel as we would have been able to return fire. We did not take them as we didn't want to make it obvious that we were carrying. Also, we did not expect to find hostility at a party full of guests.

The helicopter is closing in on us so Charles wants to find out if we anything on board to return fire. But I cannot imagine there being any weapons stored on this boat.

When they are within a few feet of us, the pilot twists the helicopter so it is facing us sideways. Then the door slides open and a gunman aims a semi-automatic rifle at us.

Charles begins to weave from left to right to avoid being hit. We see the bullets splash into the water near the boat. We continue to zig-zag as they continue to fire at us.

It is not long before they eventually hit parts of the boat which worries us. Charles shouts above the noise of the speedboat and helicopter for me to take control of the wheel. I slide behind him as he moves aside to allow me to take hold of the steering wheel.

I almost lose control of the boat as we swap position and avoid being killed.

Charles tries to find any hidden compartments that speedboats tend to have, due to small cramped spaces. He tries to see if the seat lifts up and comes forward, but nothing. He then tries the side panels, but nothing. He then checks the back of the boat where the engine is. He finally finds a small hatch that has to be a storage compartment. He fiddles with it, trying to see if it needs a key or not. He presses on it and it opens. He sees a flare gun and, for some reason, a harpoon. He ponders on which one will be more practical and cause the most damage.

I wonder what Charles is doing as I find it hard to turn round while focusing on steering left and right to dodge the bullets. I shout back at Charles asking what he is doing. He yells at me to keep the boat straight. I just make out from his voice that he has a flare gun with only one flare to shoot.

He orders me to reduce speed to allow him to steady himself more easily.

I am scared that this will give them more accuracy to shoot us. However, I do what he asks as I trust him. As we gradually reduce speed, I feel more comfortable to turn round to see where Charles is and also how close the helicopter is.

I still have to intermittently look where I am steering as I watch Charles prepare to take the shot.

I can see Charles is about to fire the flare gun when a ball of red light zooms away from us. I see the trail of smoke being created by the flare. It zig-zags vertically towards the intended target. The gunman is about to take aim as it travels towards him.

The gunman gets hit in the chest by the flare and he lights up instantly.

The flare burns through his skin and catches his clothes on fire as he panics trying to put out the flames. It is not long before the fire catches inside the helicopter.

Without any time to savour the moment and celebrate getting the gunman, there is a huge bang as the petrol tank ignites from the heat and the whole helicopter goes up in flames.

I realise that I have to push the throttle forward all the way to get distance as the helicopter falls out of the sky. We manage to avoid the debris and red ash by mere feet.

I slow the boat down to a standstill and watch the burnt shell of what is left of the helicopter slowly sink. Once it is swallowed up by the ocean, I take my time moving the boat back to shore. We travel at a comfortable cruising speed back to Charlotte Amalie.

# 13

# FOLLOW THE MONEY

We eventually get back to our hotel, mentally and physically drained. Both of us stroll through the hotel lobby in a trance. Other patrons and staff take a step back as they stare at our soaked clothes and fatigued and dazed expressions.

WHEN WE GET inside our hotel room, we get out of the damp clothes and run a bath to share. When the bath is ready, we both get in and relax in comfortable silence.

I can't quite believe that we only came here on our boss's say-so. *"Just fly over, find what happened to a politician's daughter, give him closure and fly back"*. Then go on a normal assignment.

Instead, we go to get closure with the man who caused Helen's death and he gives us key information to expose The Order and their activities. Also, we learn why we have not been able to prove their existence as their movements have been conducted through an unregulated trading platform.

We now have strong evidence to prove that they exist and also expose who the members are. I cannot believe that it has taken three years to catch a break from a second person other than Ivor.

I finish my thoughts, continue to enjoy our bath and feel more human.

WHILE WE DRY ourselves after having a long soak in the bath, we discuss the information that Epson told us. We both lie on the bed first and face each other in our complimentary bathrobes.

Charles begins the conversation with a huge sigh, 'So, now what? Pretend that we did not hear what Epson told us? Go home and get back to our normal lives of investigating companies?'

I groan to myself. 'Can we ignore it? We will only end up gathering the information, whether we go home first or go to Switzerland straight from here. Or ignore it the third time round.'

CHARLES WANTS to make sure that we persuade Miles and Mary. 'We can provide concrete proof now. If we go home, Mary will not allow us to go to Switzerland.'

I want to fly back. 'We get the next flight home first. Mull over what we need to extract, so it is not a wasted trip. Also, how do we explain to Miles that we are not going to be home for a few days? I know I got frustrated not being believed, but I just want to get it right. We are so close now. I do not want to screw it up.'

Charles understands but he wants to keep the momentum; 'If we go home, we may lose the enthusiasm to go out there and finally get the proof we need. Doubt may creep in and discourage us from following it through.'

I know he is right. 'Well, the next problem is having to tell Miles on the phone after we give him an update on what happened to Helen.'

Charles is positive; 'When we give his friend Gordon closure, Miles will be more than happy to grant us this favour. He will find it hard to say no as we helped a personal and non-related case.'

I think of the password we failed to get from Epson. 'We will need Barney help to hack into the servers to download the blockchain.'

Charles now thinks of calling our boss. 'The sooner we call Miles and conclude our assignment, the sooner we can focus on The Order.'

I WATCH Charles jump off the bed and fetch his mobile phone from on top of the desk. He rests against the desk, facing me, and flicks his mobile and taps in Miles' number. I sit up and move to the edge of the bed to be close to Charles while he speaks to Miles.

Charles puts the call on loudspeaker so both of us can hear the conversation and talk.

Miles's phone rings five times before he picks up. 'How are things going? I showed Gordon the picture you sent and confirmed that it was her. He is devastated, as you can imagine. Have you made headway?'

Charles speaks first, 'Yes. We have closure, but it has opened up a can of worms.'

Miles goes quiet for a second, then says, 'How do you mean? Have you found out how she died?'

I interrupt, 'Yes. She died on an island owned by a financier named Epson Bernstein. He was running a brothel for his mates. Trafficking underage girls.'

Miles does not sound fazed. 'Oh, hi, Jane. So, you are getting him arrested by the authorities? I will let Gordon know. I had my suspicions that her death would not be natural causes. So, get him arrested so we can put this to bed. Come home now.'

Charles squeezes his eyes shut as he goes to tell him about our new information. 'Epson is dead. He was killed by someone who wanted to shut him up. That is not all. He happened to have The Order as a client. He also knew Jane via The Order. He was instructed to frame Jane for illegal transactions. Involved Ivor.'

Miles goes quiet. 'I seem to have missed sixty seconds. This Epson guy worked for The Order, he has paperwork to frame Jane, he used Ivor to do it and now he is dead. How did he die?'

Charles sighs, 'We think The Order shut him up before we had a chance to find out everything.'

Miles is to the point, 'And did you find anything?'

Charles smiles at me, 'Yep.'

Miles goes quiet again and sighs, 'Please don't tell me you can finally prove the existence of The Order.'

Charles puts him at ease, 'We have a location where they keep their financial records. Off the books.'

Miles sounds shocked on the phone. 'Why are telling me all this?'

I spontaneously speak out, 'We could take some time off work. I have not had a holiday in months. What about you, Charles?'

Charles chortles, 'Yeah, I could do with a holiday.'

Miles sounds like he is thinking. 'I'm sure you have not completed the assignment. May need to spend another few days there. Make sure you have covered all bases.'

I feel relieved that we have the go-ahead. 'It will be a simple in and out. Grab some names and accounts. What could possibly happen?'

We finally hang up and decide to change into evening wear to go for an early dinner outside the hotel and then have an early night.

OVER DINNER, we talk more about buying an engagement ring as soon as we get back from Switzerland. Charles asks me what type of ring I would like to have. I never thought I would ever find someone to marry me let alone have a boyfriend.

I have no idea how many variations of an engagement ring you can have. I am just happy to have a ring.

We move the conversation on to our trip to Switzerland tomorrow. We get excited about gathering new information and finally getting the names of people in the society.

AFTER DINNER, it is only eight o'clock and so we decide to go to a cocktail bar. We enjoy a few drinks and get tipsy. Charles claims that he is still sober but I can tell when he is beginning to get drunk.

When we are ready to head back to the hotel, we laugh at our own conversation.

After we get back to our room, we are both too tired to have any intimacy and end up going straight to sleep.

## 14

**AND RELAX**

We arrive late in the evening at Zurich Airport, Switzerland. We take a taxi from here to Dundel where the blockchain is held. We ask the taxi driver if he has visited the place, to see if he can give us an idea of where to stay.

The driver tells us that he will drive us to a log cabin site. He assures us that there will be accommodation.

We cannot see anything outside as it is night time now. The car lights are illuminating the snowfall. Outside is -2 degrees and the driver has the climate control set at 27 degrees. It feels cosy in his car. I cuddle up to Charles as feel sleepy and ask him to wake me up when we get there.

THE TAXI DRIVER takes us to a converted farm estate. Reception is a log cabin also and we book a cabin before walking outside again. It is so cold; I wish we were in the car still.

It takes a couple of minutes to walk to our cabin.

AS SOON AS we get inside, thankfully, the cabin is already heated and warm. The log fire is already burning away and there is a metal bucket filled with spare logs.

The place is more lavish than we expected. The taxi driver chose a nice site for us to stay at. The log fire has two stools to sit in front with a thick cosy rug. They have designed this cabin for romantic get-aways.

The bed has a fur cover which I hope is fake. They have a shower and a stretched stand-alone bath. I suggest to Charles that we take a bath together to start our romantic evening, then dry naturally in front of the log fire.

Charles fancies having a hot brandy with whipped cream in the bath to go with the mood. We have a booklet listing the amenities on the site. There is a convenience store, a boutique shop, a ski shop and a restaurant. It gives us an idea to buy warmer clothes for our drive tomorrow.

While I run the bath with plenty of bubbles, Charles goes out to buy brandy and whipped cream and I ask him to buy hot chocolate.


WE SIT in the bath at opposite ends and have a side table with our hot drinks. I choose to have hot chocolate with brandy and Charles has hot neat brandy with whipped cream on top.

I manage to persuade Charles to massage my feet which makes me feel relaxed. I feel myself drifting off to sleep. As I close my eyes, Charles wants to have a conversation.

Charles is thinking about whether he is having second thoughts about tomorrow. 'Do you think we will finally find hard evidence of The Order existing and being a threat?'

I have to force myself awake by splashing water on my face. 'Once we find all the members, we can persuade Mary to investigate them individually. We can tie them all together, then leave our people to finish the leg work. Maybe get MI6 involved. We go back to what we do best.'

Charles' mind is still preoccupied, 'How did they know to kill Epson? Also, how did they get to the island so quickly? That helicopter was not your standard type.'

Too many questions to think about; 'I have no idea. I just want to enjoy our bath together.'

Charles groans at my lack of interest, 'I think it is too much of a coincidence that they came along when we were interrogating him.'

He is not going to let me relax quietly. 'They probably had his island spied on.'

Charles dwells on my comment and thinks that I could be on to something.

Eventually, we get out of the bath and sit in front of the log fire. I put treatment in my hair for half an hour before allowing my hair to dry close to the heat of the fire. Charles decides to go to bed sooner, but I want to wait until I am completely dry.


THE NEXT MORNING, we wake up after nine o'clock. I feel refreshed after having a nice relaxing bath last night and then going straight to sleep.

Charles has a shave while I get changed into a pair of jeans and a jumper. Soon, after Charles is finished getting ready, we go for breakfast.

If it were not for this site having its own amenities, we would struggle to buy what we need.

I can see why they chose this part of the world to build a blockchain as there is nothing around here. Therefore, no prying eyes to visit the building.

But I wonder where the staff live if the place is in the middle of nowhere.

After we finish breakfast, we buy warmer clothes, appropriate for this weather and get changed in our log cabin. Once we are ready to leave, we wonder where we can get a suitable car for our journey.


WE BOTH USE our mobiles to search for any sales garage or hire car place that we can go to. There does not appear to be any business for miles.

I remember seeing a Jeep parked up outside and wonder if we can borrow that. We go to reception to ask if they would know.

They are not only helpful, they offer to lend us one of the onsite maintenance vehicles. They have a black Compass Jeep.

Our route is virtually a straight road with bends and hills. We will be driving through the mountains. We also check the weather to find that we are expecting to face more snowfall, but also a light blizzard. The sat-nav on our phone gives us an estimated time of three hours.

We decide to buy food for the journey so we do not get caught short if we do not pass any service stations or fast-food outlets.


ON THE WAY out towards the mountains, there are a few residential properties outside of town. The roads are black tarmac with next to no snow settled on the road. We have agreed to share the drive with Charles driving first. The car feels so sturdy on the road that we travel at a comfortable speed of 80 mph. There is barely any other traffic on the road and so we do not have to be cautious of speed.

The road is wide enough to comfortably hold two-way traffic. Like the taxi we travelled in, the Jeep has climate control and I crank it up to 30 degrees. The seats are also heated and we used this in the beginning because the Jeep was freezing initially.

To break up the boredom, Charles uses his mobile to play the music that we like and make comfortable small talk about the scenery, and occasionally, people at work.

Based on the sat-nav, the next petrol station is about ten miles away, convenient for us to fill up as we realise we have only a quarter of a tank left.

Halfway there, we find a safe layby to stop in the mountains on the bends. I get my confidence up driving through the winding roads before I pick up speed. I am able to go as fast as 70 mph through the hilltops without feeling out of control. I have no idea how Charles had the confidence to stay at 80 mph when he drove.

Once we drive out of the mountains, the road becomes straight and that's when I push up to 90 mph to make headway.

We have been driving for two hours now and it feels like only an hour. As promised, the snow is falling but it is not affecting my vision and I can still keep a constant speed. The sky is white with no sun in sight.

We begin eating the provisions we purchased which perk me up. The roads, snow plains and mountains are continually the same and so the drive is beginning to be monotonous.

There is still no civilisation and we have not seen another car for miles. I feel the urge to reach 90 mph just to feel awake. The Jeep is quite pokey considering it is a 4 x 4, and it feels heavy.

THE SAT-NAV now says that we are five miles away. The journey leads us through a dense forest with thick white snow.

The road snakes through the woods and continues for a further few minutes. Eventually, it opens out to a huge lake with a road that is built through the middle. The road appears new with metal barriers on either side.

THE LAKE HAS a reflection of the mountains that surround the circumference. It feels calm and tranquil out here. I can see how dead calm the water is and how it is like a mirror.

We are getting closer to our destination, according to the sat-nav, with only a three-minute drive left. We can see what I think is the building for the blockchain. There is nothing else around for us to think otherwise.

We cross the lake and immediately arrive on a gravel track of dark grey slate. There is room for turning round and parking in front of the building.

THE BUILDING LOOKS like an upturned storage box. There is no window and the entrance is a single black solid metal door that is slightly sunk into the wall.

The place feels deserted as there are no other cars around. I hope we have not come here for nothing. It feels like this place is a ghost town.

We walk up to the door wondering what to expect. I check that I have my gun on me in case we face hostility at the entrance.

We see an intercom when we get closer and Charles pushes the button. I notice that there is a camera so they can see us when they answer the buzzer.

We agree that if we do not get a response, we will find a way of breaking in.

A FEW SECONDS LATER, the door opens and we glance at each other, feeling apprehensive. When we walk inside, a man welcomes us and allows us to take in the size of this place.

There is no reception area or lobby before you go into the main building.

Inside is so huge you could lose yourself. There are rows and columns of tall servers as high as the building.

I notice the ceiling is made out of glass and allows the light to come through. There are several indoor steel balconies that run around the walls of the building. There are metal stairs that you can use, or there is also a lift. I can see that each floor has a few computer desktops which must act as terminals to allow access to the blockchain.

The floor is made of grey concrete and the place lacks any degree of comfort. It also feels as cold as a warehouse.

I'm surprised we cannot see our breath.

This place is a little dark and dingy. There is a wide path in front of us that leads to the other end of the building. There is a lift that takes you to twenty floors. Each floor has a solid wall balcony with a single bar going across.

I never imagined how a network of computers would be set up. As Charles and I take in the appearance of the place, the man who let us into the building gets our attention.

The man is wearing a dark grey suit with a collarless blazer. His shirt and tie are black and he is wearing shiny slip-on shoes. He is Caucasian, tall, very slim and clean-shaven with a conservative hairstyle. He has an oblong face with black-framed glasses. His skin is slightly pale which I imagine is caused by the lack of sunlight and being cooped up in here.

He welcomes us; 'You must be here to review your general ledger.'

I put my accountant's head on. 'How many accounts can these servers hold?'

The man is proud to give us a history; 'This place was built in 2000, originally used to store weapons. But by 2001, there were budget cuts and so, it was left empty. Then someone came up with the idea of trading on a different platform. Needed a place to house the network. They guessed it would take off. So, they built the servers to handle millions of accounts. They thought big.'

I am curious to see if he knows any of the account holders. 'Do you take an interest in the names of people who hold accounts?'

The man shrugs; 'No. I just look after the place with a couple of server supporters.'

Charles asks about travelling; 'Where do you park your car? There are no houses around here for miles. I didn't see a bus stop.'

The man finds him amusing, 'We stay here in shifts. They pick us up and drop us off by helicopter.'

I wonder if anyone comes out here at all. 'How often do clients come here to look at their accounts?'

The man has to think. 'Last time was a long time ago. Hardly anyone comes here.'

We finish talking and he shows us a terminal to use to access financial records. We take the lift to reach the first floor.

WHEN WE ARE at the computer terminal, the man rattles off what we need to login and then leaves us alone. We wait for him to walk out of sight before we call Barney for his help with accessing and downloading the information and sending it directly to our agency office. As the phone dials, I take a seat in front of the terminal while Charles stands behind me and watches.

While the phone is ringing, I hope that he is not in a meeting or on a break.

BARNEY IS at his desk going through the emails he has left for a few days. He is glaring at the screen, bored out of his mind. Occasionally, he checks to see if anyone in the office is peering over his back. All he can think about is the theory he has put up on his wall at home. Also, the idea of what he thinks he knows about Jane's parents. Barney is keen to speak to Jane as soon as she gets back from her trip to the Virgin Islands, unaware that she has travelled to Switzerland.

He hears his mobile phone ring and thinks it could be his girlfriend. He glances at the mobile screen and sees it is Jane's number and answers, curious.

.  .  .

BARNEY ANSWERS my call after a few rings and I'm relieved that he picked up. Charles goes into the command screen to find the IP address. This will allow for Barney to have access to the mainframe here to download the data; better than a USB stick.

I tell Barney that we do not have time and need the names and transactions downloaded now. He understands and begins asking for the IP address and connects to the blockchain. It doesn't take him long to obtain copies of what is kept on the servers. He warns us that it will take about an hour. We just have to accept that and stand around waiting.

Barney is using his magic to download everything from the computer as we watch the screen flicker. It is like seeing a computer have a virus attack when everything shuts down. I still have Barney on the phone as he is making copies. He talks me through what percentage has been acquired so far. The download is 54% there and I check my watch to see that so far, it has taken forty minutes.

15

---

# WE'VE GOT COMPANY

Four red helicopters are inbound, approaching the roof of the building. Each helicopter is carrying four men who have been sent to kill Jane and Charles to stop them from finding the names and account numbers. They are fast approaching in pairs with the aim of going in from the roof.

When the pilots reach the building, there is not enough room for all four helicopters to dismount their crew. So, they have to take it in turns off-loading their men.

Each helicopter keeps behind one man to work a Gatling gun mounted on the side.

JANE AND CHARLES were not able to hear the helicopters above them as the roof is insulated. They are too engrossed in waiting for Barney to finish.

THREE BLACK SUVs drive across the lake and are fast approaching, with four people in each vehicle. They see the car that Jane and Charles have driven in. They block their car in case they escape the building.

They come out of their vehicles and check their guns before they go in. Then the twelve men run over to the entrance. They split up into two groups of six and line up on either side of the door. One of the men closest to the door places C4 plastic on the door.

They are ready to go inside and are waiting for the men on the roof to prepare their entrance.

Both parties are going to enter in unison as an element of surprise.

They have radio communication to give the signal.

They are all dressed in black combat clothes and carrying automatic rifles.

A total of twenty-four gunmen are getting ready to enter the building.

THE ROOF IS flat and the glass is twenty feet long and five feet wide. It is a single glass pane that is made of reinforced six-inch glass.

EACH MAN IS CARRYING a black climbing rope over their shoulder.

Once all twelve of them are on the roof, they gather around the edge of the glass. They prepare their ropes and harnesses to abseil inside the building.

Before they can go through the roof, they need to smash the glass. A couple of them pull out a few flat round black thin disks with four electrical pulsing legs attached. They fling them across the glass and have their team members place them evenly.

Once the disks are ready to activate, another of the men takes out a handheld device to activate them.

There is a quiet whistling noise that causes the glass to disintegrate into micro-particles like grains of salt.

One of them radios the men on the ground to move in now.

ROPES ARE THROWN DOWN BELOW and soon after, a dozen bodies come down like spiders in silence. The door blows open and is sent flying across the floor. Then the men coming running in using the servers as cover.

The men on the roof abseil in between the tall servers at the same time.

WE ARE stunned when we hear a loud bang and then a scraping and screeching noise. Charles walks over to the railing to see what is happening.

A FIVE-DOOR red Wrangler Jeep comes hurtling towards the blockchain, travelling at over a hundred miles an hour. It is nothing to do with the party that have arrived already. It is Stellar Star driving in a purpose-built armoured car.

She has been following the same breadcrumb trail but a couple of hours behind. She has no idea what she will be facing when she arrives there.

When she arrives, she drifts the car in a circle before yanking the handbrake up and skidding to a halt.

WHEN SHE COMES out of the car, she stretches her arms in the air and exaggerates a yawn. She is wearing black combat trousers and laced black military boots. She has a black blouse with a black sleeveless puffer jacket.

She assesses her surroundings and stares at the three SUVs. Then she notices that the door has been blown off.

She casually walks around the back of her car and opens the door. There is nothing in the back. She slides her finger along the edge of the bumper where the boot begins. A faint L.E.D blue light follows her finger. Then a whirring motor sounds as the floor of the boot flips over. There she can see an array of assault weapons; semi-automatic rifles, knives, stun grenades and handguns. She has not come empty-handed.

Stellar grabs two of the three semi-automatics, two handguns and three stun grenades. Once she is happy with her choice of weapons, she casually walks over to the entrance.

BARNEY IS NOW near to completing the full upload of the names and banks accounts on the blockchain.

While I wait for the upload to complete, I take a brief glimpse at transactions coming in and out. I cannot believe how much money The Order has and how big they are.

Charles is not impressed and walks over to the edge of the floor and stares at the size of the servers.

I CANNOT HELP BEING MESMERISED by how good Barney is at his job after all these years. I think he is amazing at his work.

Before I know it, the transfer is complete when I see 100% appear on the computer screen. We can finally leave this place and head home.

Barney can analyse the information before we arrive home. I am relieved that we do not have to carry the physical data ourselves. I would be too nervous to lose a USB stick after all this effort retrieving the data.

.  .  .

I WONDER what Charles is finding interesting and turn round to find out. He appears to be searching for something down below. I ask what he has seen but he is distracted.

As I go to turn back round, we hear gunfire from the ground and Charles gets his gun out. He runs towards me and I bolt up off the seat. I take my gun out and wonder what we do now.

While we can hear continual gunfire below, the lift pings and we face the frame of the doors and wait for it to open.

Charles spontaneously shouts at me to drop to the floor. As I drop to the floor, three armed men come out and open fire. We both return fire and the three men are instantly killed.

We head for the stairs to run down to the ground floor.

WHILE WE RUN down the stairs, we notice the same black woman from the island here. We are distracted by her skills and I notice Charles admiring her. I close his mouth for him and tell him that her talent is nothing to be impressed by.

STELLAR IS single-handedly taking on the remaining twenty bad guys as she weaves in and out of the servers. She stops firing to focus on their footsteps to work out where they are. She hides behind a server and waits for them to approach her.

The remaining eleven men think they know where she is and split into two groups and gather from either side towards her.

Stellar takes out four stun grenades and rolls them, one behind her, then on her left and right. She then waits for the grenades to ignite.

The gunmen are instantly dazed by the flash and are disorientated. Stellar comes out of hiding and begins taking them out as she fires at them.

A handful of them drop to the ground like a guillotine.

WE REALISE that we are only halfway down the stairs and begin momentum to help the woman out. I fire a few rounds off to get their attention away from her.

The eight remaining men scurry off for cover which leaves us a window to escape out of the building. The woman sees us and follows behind.

.   .   .

WHEN WE ARE OUTSIDE, the black woman runs away from us and I can see a car in her direction. We run to our car but quickly realise that ours is blocked by the gunmen.

The woman shouts at us to come with her. Charles and I stare at one another, puzzled as to why she is happy to take us with her when she has no idea about us. She barks at us again and we feel obliged to tag along with her even though we have no idea who she is.

We can see that she has a cherry-red Jeep parked at an angle, facing towards us. I watch her go into the left side of the car. She orders me to get in the other side and Charles in the back.


WHEN ALL THREE of us are in the car, I realise she is expecting me to drive. I fiddle with the steering column presuming there is a car key.

As I struggle to work out how to start the car, we see the remaining eight men running out of the entrance and begin firing at us.

I crouch down hoping that they do not disable the car to prevent our escape. The woman, whose name we still do not know, is cool as a cucumber.

As the hail of bullets comes towards us, I hear the sound like the patter of fat droplets of rain as the bullets hit the shell of the Jeep. There are no marks on the windows or the metal body of the bonnet.

Charles pretends to be aware of the car being armour-plated as he composes himself, acting normal.

The woman calmly reassures us, 'It is okay, she's bullet-proof. By the way, my name is Stellar Star. Yours?'

I answer first, 'Knight. Jane Knight.'

Charles casually says his name, 'May, Charles May.'

Stellar sees the men begin to run towards us. 'I suggest you push the button on the side of the steering column. I have the key in my pocket.'

I push the button and it roars alive. I shove the automatic gear into drive and floor the car when the men are within a couple of feet. The wheels judder as they find their grip.


I SPIN the car round to drive towards the lake. Slate is flying behind us as I push the accelerator to the floor.

I briefly check the car out and see that the dashboard has a 12-inch screen that mimics your mobile phone screen. It also has a built-in camera for the back of the car as well as a sat-nav.

I check the rear-view mirror to see eight men scramble to their three SUV cars.

.   .   .

WHILE WE DRIVE along the lake, out of nowhere, two helicopters are hovering at car level on either side of us. I see the three pursuers behind us in single file and a third helicopter hovering behind the third car. We are travelling at over 100 mph and struggling to gain distance from them.

I jump when I see a fourth helicopter come down in front of us hovering widthways.

I have no idea how we are going to get out of this one. We are stuck on the lake for a further five minutes before we are given cover by the wooded road.

Charles and Stellar seem to be undisturbed and Charles is sat back enjoying the ride.

The three SUVs begin firing at us and I can see trails of fireflies heading toward us. The bullets have no effect on the car though.

While we are being shot at, in the helicopter on our left, the side door slides open and a heavy-duty machine gun appears and begins firing.

I feel the car drifting from the impact and compensate the steering to keep straight. At this rate, we are not going to survive this. But Stellar shows no panic in her face and sees this as a normal day. Charles is twitchy even though he is relaxed.

I watch her touching the screen on the dashboard and see the menus flickering. A few seconds later, she has the screen showing us a backward view of the black SUVs chasing us. I see her smile to herself as she pushes a button.

Something is happening and I'm not sure what. I check in the rear-view mirror to see a brown slush spreading along the road behind us.

I can hear Stellar quietly laughing and getting excited. I watch the car behind us begin to lose control as it swerves and eventually skids off the road. It smashes through the road barrier and crashes into the lake. The water engulfs the car and it sinks below the surface.

The next car is already sliding about but the driver keeps control. Stellar shows frustration and pushes a few more buttons. The next thing I see is flame leaving the back of the Jeep. The slush catches fire and the front of the car eventually gets engulfed in flames. The driver cannot see through the flames engulfing the bonnet and windscreen. It is not long before the SUV explodes into a ball of flames. There is only one car left now that smashes through the burnt-out car, causing debris to fly everywhere.

The helicopter to our left is still continually firing at us. The other two helicopters join in and we are being hit in all directions. Stellar continues to play with the screen.

Charles is calm and does not acknowledge how great he thinks Stellar is.

I continue to stare into the rear-view mirror to see where the remaining car is. I watch the driver smash through the burnt-out car and send discarded matter through the air. The helicopter flies through the debris soon after.

We are still being pursued by the two helicopters on either side of us and now both of them are firing at us.

Stellar is glancing to either side at the helicopters and begins playing with the screen.

I wonder what else this Jeep can do. 'Is there anything that this car has that we can use to get rid of these helicopters?'

Stellar is too preoccupied to respond, 'Charles. Can you move to your left a little? Thanks, babe.'

Charles has a puzzled expression. 'Sure, ma-am. Anything else I can do for you? Rub your shoulders?'

Stellar finds him amusing. 'Yes. But later though.'

The next thing that happens is that the middle section of the Jeep, in front of the gear stick and handbrake, opens up. I cannot believe my eyes when I see a cannon begin whirring vertically upwards and a mid-section of the hard roof unfold.

There is a clang as the cannon fully extends. I notice that the screen changes image and I can see the road in front with an image of a white target. I watch Stellar use the control dials and the camera moves with the cannon. She aims the gun at the helicopter to our left. When the target is clear, the white target blips to red. She aims the gun at the pilot and when Stellar is ready, she pushes the dial.

A jet of ammunition takes out the pilot and makes the helicopter fly out of control. It weaves about and eventually swerves into the SUV behind us and both instantly combust on impact. The force from the explosion jolts us forward

Now, there are only the other two helicopters left, one on our right and one in front. Stellar controls the gun to face the helicopter in front. There is quite a bit of distance between us and the helicopter. Stellar has to zoom the camera to get a closer aim.

Once she has her target, she pushes the same dial and a burst of ammunition flies at the man controlling the Gatling gun. The power of our cannon is no match for the gunman and tears the Gatling apart. Eventually, the helicopter begins to slowly disintegrate until it crashes to the ground. There is a huge explosion that blocks the road.

I am approaching the remains of the helicopter too fast. I do not have time to manoeuvre around the burning heap of twisted metal. I shout out to Charles and Stellar to hold on tight. I floor the car to hit this burning helicopter head on to drive through it. I close my eyes at the last minute and scream out loud. Stellar braces herself with her hand on the dashboard and there is a huge bang and I feel the Jeep drive into the mangled metal. I open my eyes and we are already through the carnage. I check the rear-view mirror and wonder how we did not go up in flames.

WE ARE FINALLY past the lake and head along the winding road through the snowy forest. There is only one helicopter left to worry about.

The pilot has to ascend as the rotor blades are too wide for the trees. Stellar is not able to angle the cannon and so we cannot take it out.

It is hard to keep a constant speed of 100 mph with the sharp bends. We cannot see the helicopter anymore and assume that it has given up the ghost.

Just as we think that, the road straightens up briefly and the helicopter is sat on the road with the wheels down. It fires at us instantly and, as I begin to lose my nerve, Stellar shouts at me to speed up. She plays with the touch screen again and I hear a whirring noise coming from the front of the car.

Stellar softly speaks to herself, 'Just a few more seconds. Steady.'

Her forefinger hovers over the dial and is poised.

Stellar is still poised, 'Steady. Steady. Goodbye.'

With that, she pushes the button and a rocket fires out from the left headlight and a trail of white smoke follows.

The pilot struggles to pull up in time and there is an instant explosion. I do not have the guts to drive through another burning helicopter, so I slam the brakes on and yank the steering wheel and slide to a halt.

It is over.

# 16

# THE NEXT MOVE

The three of us are back at our log cabin. I have already spoken to Barney since we arrived back. He has confirmed that from the blockchain, he has accessed all the original transactions of all the account names and bank account numbers.

He tells us that he has uploaded this onto our servers as the file is too big for desktop storage and we do not have external hard drives large enough.

He briefly mentions that he has found a link between the blockchain ledger and bank accounts at a bank in Cuba. All the funds are filtered in 'Banco Nacional de Cuba', in Cayman Island waters. It will be a tax haven country and a place no one in the intelligence community would think to search. Also, the bank would appear to be owned and controlled by The Order.

BARNEY IS EXCITED to have concrete data to support his theory of The Order's strategy and is now ready to approach Miles and Mary with the information. Before he goes to them, he wants to put his idea in methodical order with supporting evidence, tidy up his notes and make a Power-Point presentation. Then he wants to run the idea by one of his colleagues before he shows them. He wants to get a non-biased opinion of his findings before he goes to Miles and Mary.

He is keen to finish work in the next few hours so he can head home to do that.

. . .

THE THREE OF us are sat around a four-seater table discussing what our next move is. Stellar draws a blank as she hoped to get the same data as us, but we had company and so she could not get her own copy.

We formally introduce ourselves and explain how we both ended up on Epstein island.

Charles speaks for both of us; 'We work for an intelligence organisation called The Agency. I am a former MI6 agent. We investigate companies that are a threat to English soil, mainly filthy rich CEOs who fund terrorist groups. Our boss had an informer that he passed on to Jane to help put away a man called Vladimir Mashkov. Our informer goes by the name of Ivor Peteski. We have not spoken to him in three years. He is a part of The Order but keeps his distance and is kept out of the loop.'

Stellar questions our faith in Ivor. 'How do you know he is a reliable source?'

Chares continues, 'We know. He has helped us out a few times. We have found out about The Order's existence through him. But it was having the proof to back it up. How about your background and how you found out that The Order existed?'

Stellar shares her past first; 'I work for an agency that you would have heard of before, Defence In All Manner Of National and Domestic Security; D.I.A.M.O.N.D.S for short.'

Charles is more clued up with the global intelligence community and adds, 'I'm sure you are. But no. I assume you are not government-funded.'

Stellar confirms, 'That would be correct. It is funded by some wealthy people in the private sector. They wanted an agency to protect their financial interests. Not for personal gain. Hence the expensive toys. I know governments plead austerity. Also, they care about their own agenda.'

I like the sound of D.I.A.M.O.N.D.S already. 'I assume you will be around forever?'

Stellar is not amused by my attempt at humour. 'Like I have not heard that a million times.'

Charles is wondering, 'Diamond in the rough. How did you get on the trail of The Order?'

Stellar finds his comment amusing, 'We came across The Order when we realised that we had a mole in our agency; a spy among us. We sensed a threat that we decided to look into. We seemed to be a step behind. We had our suspicions about one particular guy, Mr Black. We created a fictitious breakthrough with a piece of new information. We put it on a secure server. We gave the access to only one person, someone we trusted. And someone hacked in. We traced their digital print to a Mr Black. By the time we exposed him, he had done a runner. I caught up with him in Brazil. I terminated his contract permanently. But before I killed him, he begged for his life and he gave me Epson Bernstein who looked after their financial investments.'

Now that we have both given a brief history of how we stumbled on The Order, I mention what conversation I had with our IT guy, Barney, back in London. I explain that we have found that they hold all the accounts in Cuba, in the capital city, Havana.

I feel the urge to take a trip down there before we head back home to England. Stellar is keen to come with me and Charles is obliged to agree to come with us.

The conversation changes back to Mr Black, and Charles and I are intrigued as to how he knew Epson.

I bring up the question, 'How did Mr Black and Epson meet?'

Stellar recounts what she found out. 'Mr Black and Epson knew each other from university. Epson got him involved in regards to getting him a job. The last thing he thought was that he would be spying on behalf of them.'

Charles wonders how she found him. 'What made you think he was in Brazil?'

Stellar recounts how she found him. 'At first, it was hard to work out where he could have gone. It was finding his known associates and if they knew his whereabouts. I followed several leads that ended up being dead-ends. Then, I caught a break when my people in Brazil spotted him.'

Charles is curious, 'How long did it take to track him down?'

Stellar thinks back. 'Two years. In between other assignments.'

I think out loud, 'Two years. That must have been soul-destroying not knowing if you would ever find him. Even after a year or six months.'

Stellar sighs and rolls her eyes, 'Tell me about it. My motivation was wanting to ring his neck for having the audacity to spy on us. How long have you known about The Order?'

I choose to answer the question; 'Four years. But it went stale for three until we ended up learning about Epson.'

Stellar is curious about how we found Epson, 'So, how did you end up on the island? I assume Epson told you about her.'

I concur with her last comment; 'We were originally sent to investigate the disappearance of a politician's daughter. It was a favour for our boss who knows her father. The enquiry and evidence led to Epson's island. We found out she was pimped out to his rich friends. He was a sex trafficker.'

Stellar is open-mouthed. 'I didn't get that far finding out about Epson. How is the girl? Did you find her in the end?'

I feel sad as I tell her, thinking it could have been one of my nieces. 'She died from an overdose, on the island.'

Stellar wishes she had not asked. 'I'm sorry.'

Charles concludes, 'She died of a drug overdose, supplied by her employer. I frazzled his balls in return.'

Stellar expresses her approval of his method. 'Good. It was worth not having a chance to interrogate him.'

Charles wonders where she went when we were being chased. 'We ran outside and we could not see you. Where did you disappear to?'

Stellar recalls what she did, 'I saw the helicopter shoot up the house. My people followed me to the island and waited for me on the other side. I got my ride that way. We did not see the helicopter or you. I saw the man you were with taking care of the guests and getting off the island.'

WHEN WE FINISH INTRODUCING ourselves with our background and knowledge on The Order, we all agree to go to Cuba. We will go to 'Banco Nacional de Cuba' to find out how much money they have to fund their cause. Also, to find out if any of the accounts show trading in the UK.

Stellar wants to have copies of what we found at the site today. We are more than happy to share our information to stop their plans.

THE NEXT MORNING, we head back to Zurich Airport, hoping that we can find a flight to Cuba. It is another hour and a half drive to the airport.

Stellar drives and I sit in the back while Charles sits in the front. It feels weird travelling in a car that is full of gadgets. I thought they were only in movies. I did not realise that certain agencies had the money to build this kind of cars.

I wish that our agency could afford to supply us with a fully-loaded car. Instead, we only have mobile phones with apps that any civilian can buy online themselves, except for the add-ons that Barney supplies. I think I am jealous of her having whatever she wants to complete her missions.

Charles' eyes wander over the dashboard, wondering what else this car can do. Stellar occasionally slaps Charles' hand away when he tries to fiddle with the dials and touch screen.

He is like a child in a sweet shop wanting to try everything.

WHEN WE ARRIVE IN ZURICH, Stellar parks in the multi-storey car park for her people to collect it.

We go to one of the booking desks to arrange a flight to Cuba for three. We are even willing to upgrade to first class which is less fully booked.

When we are happy to pay for upper-class seats, there is no problem finding seats.

We pay with the credit cards supplied by our agencies.


DURING OUR FLIGHT, we use the time to catch up on sleep. We are happy in our comfortable silence. We have seats next to each other with Stellar on my right and Charles on my left. I adjust my body so I can lean on Charles' shoulder for a pillow and fall asleep.

We have a fourteen-hour flight to reach Cuba.

# 17

# WELCOME TO CUBA

Xavier is pruning his flowers near the swimming pool while he quietly hums to himself. He finds this exercise relaxing and calming. He is dressed casually in an untucked white shirt and white trousers instead of his usual suit. He has no work schedule today and is using this time to enjoy being away from work.

His assistant comes out of the mansion, walking briskly down the white steps towards the flower beds.

He is Caucasian with olive skin, in his thirties, with dark brown hair, and a thin trimmed beard.

He is worried about what his employer's reaction will be when he passes on the sad news. He is nervous about receiving the response from Xavier as he is aware of his bad temper.

He approaches Xavier nervously and waits for him to acknowledge his presence. Xavier knows why he is there and knows it is not good news. Attending to his flowers is not making him calm.

His assistant cannot bear the silence and speaks up, 'There is a problem.'

Xavier raises his hand and points his finger up to motion him to stop. His assistant pauses nervously as he knows when Xavier is going to lose his rag.

Xavier continues to prune his rose tree with no expression. 'I take it you have come to tell me that they are still alive.'

His assistant replies with a nervous voice, 'They had unexpected help.'

Xavier sighs as he makes no eye contact. 'Any survivors?'

His assistant knows how he is going to react, 'Um, it would appear there were no survivors.'

Xavier sucks his lips inwards to control his temper. 'Do we know who the person was who joined the party?'

His assistant is fidgety as he does not have good news. 'We have no record on her.'

Xavier changes the conversation; 'Where are they heading now?'

His assistant worries about his reaction. 'They are heading to Cuba. I believe they are heading to the bank that holds all the accounts and names of the heads of families involved in The Order. I don't have to tell you the rest. They will discover our plans, the size of the organisation, not to mention how much we are worth.'

Xavier chortles to himself, 'You think? Round up some more men. This time, don't miss. They will have their mystery friend there. Tell them that if they fail and the three survive, don't bother coming back. The next time you come to update me, don't bother if it is not good news.'

His assistant knows he means that. 'Yes.'

Xavier is not finished; 'There are guns for hire in Bosnia and Herzegovina. We will need them to destroy the data they have already at the MI6 building.'

His assistant has his own thoughts; 'Our contact will need to give them a blueprint of the building and provide access.'

Xavier already knows, so tells him, 'I will have someone converse with them.'

HALFWAY THROUGH THE FLIGHT, we are awake and decide to go to the drinks bar upstairs.

The three of us stand by the bar and there are only a couple of other people drinking alone. We each choose an alcoholic drink, with Charles ordering neat rum, Stellar having vodka and coke and me trying peach-flavoured gin.

There is more I want to know about Stellar, so I ask, 'Which part of America do you live in?'

Stellar sips her drink before she answers; 'Los Angeles.'

I want to know more about her. 'How did you end up working for D.I.A.M.O.N.D.S?'

Stellar takes another sip of her vodka and coke before saying, 'I was in the Navy at first. My father was in the Navy. I was trained in being a sniper and then went into special ops. Did that for a few years until I felt it was time to move on. I did two tours in Iraq. When I left, I got head-hunted when the organisation began to expand. To carry out my work, they supply me with the latest gadgets.'

I envy her; 'I wish our government would do the same. But they come up with austerity.'

Stellar almost laughs; 'Yeah. We have the same thing with our government. But privately owned intelligence agencies do not have that issue.'

Charles wonders what other toys she has available. 'So, what support will you have available in Cuba?'

Stellar orders another vodka and coke. 'I won't have the car. All I will have are my guns and some toys inside my luggage.'

Stellar asks me about my background; 'How did you end up working for The Agency?'

I think back and it seems like light-years away. 'I never imagined myself being a civil servant. I was an accountant for a practice firm in London. I met my boss at an engagement party. Before I knew it, he was testing me out.'

Stellar is curious to know how, so she asks, 'What did he ask you to do?'

I recollect what happened. 'He asked me to look into a few financial accounts and interpret the figures. I confirmed to him which company was most likely financing terrorists.'

Stellar admires me. 'Your pretty much a geek. What made you say yes to being an industrial spy?'

I do not want to tell the truth, so I just say, 'I wanted a change. Saw it as an escape from my dull boring life. Told it would be an adventure.'

Stellar senses something is not quite right. 'There seems to be more to it.'

I do not feel comfortable having this discussion in front of Charles. 'Why do you think that?'

Charles can see that I do not want to talk about it, so he butts in; 'Her parents died around the same time and she felt she needed a change.'

I do not want to go into detail as I had a choice of the possibility of suicide or joining The Agency. A change of scenery would stop me from going ahead.

I do not want Stellar knowing that. Charles knows everything about me and so he knows about my attempt before joining.

After Charles' response about my parents dying, Stellar does not force the question.


WHEN WE FINALLY REACH CUBA, landing at José Martí International Airport, and by the time we go through customs and collect our luggage, it is after eight o'clock in the morning. We then head to the taxi rank.

Stellar tells us that she has allies here and plans to see them before we leave to go home to our respective places. Stellar seems to have a cultural connection with Cubans, so she takes the lead and arranges which hotel to stay in. She directs us where to find a taxi and where to drive to.

.   .   .

WE STAY at the 'Gran Hotel Manzana Kempinski La Habana' which is a six-star hotel costing $1,000 a night. We arrive at the hotel before nine o'clock.

The hotel overlooks the ocean and a long stretch of beachfront. We are staying in one suite with space for three.

We are struggling to fight through the jetlag and so we decide to go for a long rest. We have a feeling that our visit to the bank will go smoothly.

The hotel suite has two bedrooms so Charles and I, naturally, share the twin room while Stellar has the double room.


I WAKE up naturally and feel like it is late afternoon, around four o'clock. I check my phone and see it is 4.13 pm. I roll over to face Charles and cannot help but stare at him. I cannot believe that we are going to be officially engaged when we get back home. I have been wondering what type of ring I would like. I can hear him breathing and find it comforting.

I begin to imagine us getting married and inviting my friends who are married already and have children. The thought of picturing us walking up the aisle after tying the knot makes me feel in the mood for intimacy.

I reach under the sheets and feel for his manhood. As I gently rub him, I can see him stirring as he gets hard between my fingers. For a second, I imagine Stellar opening the door as we go to make love and hope that she knocks first.

I watch Charles stirring from his sleep and briefly smile as I feel him in the palm of my hand getting aroused. I never get bored of getting him turned on. I hear him murmur while he keeps his eyes closed.

He turns over onto his back and parts his legs as I begin to work him up and down. I find myself smiling as Charles quietly groans as my rhythm speeds up. As his groan grows louder, I quickly dart my eyes at the door hoping that Stellar is asleep.

I then turn to the sheets as I see my hands shuffling underneath and notice Charles begin to stiffen. The next moment, I see the sheet go wet and feel warm liquid run down my fingers. I keep stroking him to see if he still has some cum left to release. Then, I wipe my hands clean underneath the sheets.

Charles wants to return the favour but we hear Stellar through the door. So, we go for a shower to freshen up and see what Stellar wants to do.

.   .   .

IT IS NOW six o'clock and the day has gone. We decide that we would like to go out for a few drinks this evening. Between us, we search the internet on our mobile phones. There is a cocktail bar within walking distance from here, along the beach.

Charles wears a pair of trousers and a short-sleeved shirt which he leaves untucked. I wear a pair of shorts and a short-sleeved blouse. As we come out of our bedroom, Stellar walks out of hers and we realise we are wearing similar clothes. We glance at each other and then at ourselves. My other shorts are similar and so I have no other choice.

We all drink the same as we take it in turn to choose the next colourful cocktail. The music is making us feel in the mood to dance.

Charles and I are too relaxed to hide our relationship as we seductively dance together and enjoy the music. The alcohol makes us lose our inhibitions and we end up kissing passionately and giggling together.

Stellar stays at the bar and we can see her staring at us as she is happy to continue drinking.

Cuba is a great place, but I had never considered coming here for a holiday. There is a vibrant atmosphere and the locals are friendly.

We stay out till after one o'clock in the morning.

THE NEXT MORNING, I wake up to see that Charles is not in bed. I can hear indistinct chatter through the door and get up to see what they are up to.

I feel groggy but with no hangover and craving for breakfast. Somehow, I managed to dress myself in my pyjamas when we arrived back.

When I open the door, I see that Charles and Stellar have ordered breakfast already. They ordered enough for me as well.

I wonder what our plans are; 'When are we going to the bank?'

Charles already has our itinerary laid out. 'We are going to the bank late afternoon. Now, we are going to D.I.A.M.O.N.D.S' office that is downtown. And, we will see what else this place has to offer.'

Stellar gets her luggage out of her bedroom and places it on the table in the living area. Charles and I watch her open it up and take her belongings out. I am curious to see what she is doing. She next rips out the soft fabric interior. Then she takes out parts of what seems like a state-of-the-art rifle. After that come the explosives. She is not messing as she puts together her automatic rifle.

Charles is curious to know what she is expecting; 'What are you doing with a high-calibre rifle? And how are you going to walk out with that through reception?'

Stellar eyes the length of the barrel. 'I will take it apart again. I think we are going to face hostility. Your spy will have already told them we are here. If they are everywhere, then I promise you, they are already here. I am expecting World War Three.'

I am speechless. 'Well, for their sake, let's hope they are not here.'

Charles is surprised to think that we will face hostility; 'No one knows we are here except for Barney. We have not spoken to anyone else. How could The Order possibly know we are in Cuba?'

Stellar is not changing her theory. 'Trust me. They are here. Mr Black piggybacked off our calls and computers. Someone in your office is feeding back to them.'

I am with Charles and say, 'That is impossible. I know everyone in the office. Even our boss, Miles, is astute and he would know if he'd hired an enemy. We also have a well-experienced woman who heads The Agency. She is a good judge of character.'

Charles admires my argument as he turns away, 'Absolutely.'

Stellar is still sticking to her belief; 'Well, you believe what you think and I will believe what I know. Ask me this, at any point when investigating this society have you ever had unexpected company?'

Our thoughts are blank in regards to Stellar's question. She slowly shakes her head in disbelief while she continues checking her rifle.

Stellar tries to think of another way to phrase her question; 'When was your last assignment involving The Order?'

I think back three years ago, 'Back when we were after an escapee who had connections to The Order.'

Stellar asks about our assignment; 'Did you have opposition during your assignment?'

Charles thinks back. 'Your sister's house was destroyed. Only Miles knew where we were. When we were being chased on the highway in Florida; that was odd.'

Stellar shrugs her shoulders; 'There you go. We are going to steal important names and bank accounts. They are not going to lie down while we steal sensitive information.'

I guess she is right and I make a proposition; 'So, we go in armed to the teeth. Then, we go home and find the spy among us.'

Charles agrees. 'Will your people lend us some toys?'

Stellar smiles, 'Absolutely.'

Charles squints his eyes at her, 'That's my line.'

Now we have considered that we may face problems, the idea of waltzing into the bank sounds daunting. But this also means that we are getting closer to them.


AFTER HAVING BREAKFAST, we leave the hotel to go to her Cuban division by taxi. Her agency office is a couple of miles away.

Stellar is sat in the front while Charles and I are holding hands in the back like we are going on a date. I feel unprofessional with her knowing that we are an item and not just agency partners. Charles does not seem to be fazed by her knowing.

Stellar turns round to see that we are holding hands and smiles at us before turning back. She makes me feel weird for having a boyfriend.

I distract myself from my thoughts by watching the taxi driver weaving in and out of stationary cars, beeping at people crossing the road in front of us. The driver is quiet while he is focusing on the road.

The windows are all half-open as the car does not have air conditioning. It is an old classic New York taxi cab.

The sky is bright blue with the sun baking down and I already feel hot and bothered. My back feels like it is beginning to be soaked in sweat.

After ten minutes in the car, we finally arrive at our destination. The taxi driver pulls up a narrow road with tall apartment buildings on either side in a quiet part of town. There is no one around and we cannot work out if we are in an affluent area or a middle-class one.

WHEN WE GET out of the car, there is an old worn door opposite where we have stopped. It appears uninhabited.

We follow Stellar across the road as the taxi driver leaves. She bangs on the metal door with her fist three times. A few seconds later, when there is no response, Stellar glances up, glaring at a camera that is dated and seems broken.

We then hear a clank and a clunk and the door is opened from within. It is initially dark inside as we walk in.

The lights above us begin to blink on like they are activated by sensors. When we can see, the interior does not reflect the tired appearance of the outside.

There are two levels with a platform upstairs overlooking the ground. The floor is made out of dark brown wood.

D.I.A.M.O.N.D.S' office is open-plan with chrome office chairs and glass desks. The decor is contemporary with neutral-coloured painted walls like some buildings are in the city.

Staff are too busy working to take notice of us. Stellar leads us up the stairs to the top floor. As we reach the top, one of her colleagues greets us and asks who Charles and I are.

After a few minutes of introducing each other, Stellar asks her colleague if we could talk in private.

. . .

WE WALK over to a corner of the floor that is the closest we are going to get
to privacy. Her colleague's name is Aleja Fernández, and she is in her mid-
thirties with a sheen to her flawless brown skin. She is tall and slim,
wearing a grey sleeveless tailored office dress with black matt-finish high
heels. She is wearing a pair of black-rimmed oblong glasses. They suit her
slim high cheekbones.

The three of us take a seat with nothing between us.

Stellar wants to make a courtesy call as she is in the area. 'How long
has it been?'

Aleja thinks, 'Three years ago? When we went dancing till five in the
morning.'

Stellar's memory comes flooding back to that night; 'Ah yes. Quite a
night. How are things down Cuba?'

Aleja sits back in her chair. 'We were able to help the local drug
agency round up a supply chain. From here to Miami and Honduras. And
we helped to bust a credit card fraud. How about you?'

Stellar brings up our current assignment. 'We are tracking a society.
We have been led here. I need some supplies.'

Aleja has a quizzical expression. 'Who are you going to upset now?'

Stellar tries not to smile as she says, 'In case negotiations do not go
well.'

Aleja smirks and winks at her. 'Follow me.'


WE FOLLOW Aleja downstairs and head towards the back to a glass door
which she takes us through.

I cannot believe how many rows and rows of guns they have. They
could support a small army. Aleja also has some additional gadgets that
she shows us, kept in a row of metal drawers. She pulls out a few drawers
until she finds what she wants to show us.

She gives us each a black compact bag the size of a folded cagoule. I
stare at it with confusion until we are told that we throw it down at the
ground. I still do not get it but Charles and Stellar seem to know what it
does. However, they do not explain and so I pretend to understand so I do
not feel stupid.

We are also given a few explosives each that are powerful enough to
blow a hole in a wall as thick as two feet. We are also given a man bag to
put them in.

Before we go, Stellar asks for a car to drive. Aleja ponders on her question and eventually walks us outside the back of the building to a car
park. There are a few employee cars that are run of the mill. They have a
pool car that anyone can use for work purposes. It is a vintage BMW five-
door in silver. It is an older version of a 1972 BMW 2002 tii.

We cannot believe how old the car is and Aleja is pleased to hand over the key as she chortles while walking away. Charles takes the key and Stellar pushes me aside to get into the passenger side. I begrudgingly get in the back of the car.

We set off for 'Banco Nacional de Cuba'.

## With A Bang

WE DRIVE through a narrow alleyway from behind D.I.A.M.O.N.D.S' building to reach the main road. We are ten minutes away from the bank as Charles drives us through the busy roads. I can hear the gears crunching while Charles is getting used to driving this old car. I feel myself being jolted about in the back as there is no seat belt.

You can feel every bump in the road with the suspensions creaking occasionally.

THERE ARE a group of motorcyclists dressed all in black leather and helmets, on souped-up motorbikes, carrying gun holsters. There are eight of them travelling towards their target along the A4, reaching the outskirts of Havana. One of them in front is leading the pack and tracking Jane and Charles' mobile signal.

As they ride through the built-up area, you can hear the echoing sound of their engines revving through the city.

Tourists and locals are distracted from their itinerary as they glance at the riders when they zoom past them.

A pedestrian walks along a crossing in the road and, halfway over, is frozen to the spot as the eight motorbikes race either side of him. The person jumps as they feel the rush of air rushing past their body.

CHARLES IS DRIVING like we are in a scene from 'Driving Miss Daisy', happily dawdling along the road as if we have all the time in the world. It feels so hot in the car was the fan is broken. All the windows are down but that does not make any difference.

Stellar has her elbow resting on the door seal, not breaking a sweat. The seat is old worn red leather that makes you feel uncomfortably hot.

Glancing in the rear-view mirror, I catch sight of Charles staring at me and finding it amusing that I am so uncomfortable. While Charles continues to glance at me occasionally, something distracts him and his eyes see past me. I naturally turn round to see what is catching his eye. When I turn round, I notice, in the distance, a group of motorbikes. At first, I think nothing of it until I realise they are going quite fast and approaching us at great speed.

I know that something is wrong and feel the car jolt forward and pick up speed. Stellar also senses that we are going to have conflict.

I get my gun out and prepare to return fire if they are not passing through. The car is struggling to travel over eighty miles an hour and it feels like this car will tear itself apart.

I see Stellar already poised with her gun facing in my direction. Charles is focusing his stare in the mirror at the bikers heading closer towards us.

Charles talks through his idea; 'I am going to drive along the beach-front. The roads here are busy and narrow. We will stand a better chance on the open road. You were right, Stellar; we have a mole. But I don't know how they managed to find some vigilantes in Cuba.'

I wonder the same, 'Well, as soon as we get back, we let Miles and Mary know.'

Stellar is not concerned. 'Let's gets out of this first. We get rid of these bikers before we head to the bank. How fast can this thing go?'

Charles smiles and drops down a gear to give some oomph and the engine squeals under the strain.

I critique D.I.A.M.O.N.D.S' choice of pool car; 'I thought you guys had money?'

Stellar is still waiting for the bikers to reach us. 'We don't exactly have a variety of flashy cars in Cuba. Besides, what's wrong with this ride?'

I do not respond and focus on what is about to happen.


WE FINALLY REACH the road that stretches the length of the beach. As we turn left onto the wide road, the bikers pull out their guns and prepare to fire at us.

Stellar and I duck as the back windscreen shatters and I get covered in small shards of glass. The rear-view mirror is also shot off.

A few seconds later, Stellar and I both return fire, failing to make a hit. The bikers swerve in single file and avoid our bullets. They spread out and continue to try and kill us with firepower. Neither side is winning. Before we know it, two of them flank us on either side and are about to take a shot. I aim for the right and Stellar goes for the other.

I see Stellar smile at the biker like she wants to sleep with him and then shoots one round off and the biker dies instantly. I lean out of the car window and shoot the other rider at the same time. The car is swerving about as Charles tries to shake him off. As I go to fire, I feel the wheels hit a bump and it causes me to squeeze the trigger. I end up taking out their back tyre and he instantly loses control. The bike veers off and slams into an ice cream van across the road. I see the ice cream man getting forced through the serving window.

A few seconds later, the van goes up with a kaboom. I guess the motorcyclist got creamed.

Charles is getting fed up. 'We are going to get killed on this road. At the next junction, I am going to yank the steering wheel away from the beach. I am going to slow down.'

Stellar is stunned, 'You what?!'

When we reach the next available turning, Charles takes it and the car screeches as we drift into what we think is a road. It turns out to be a pedestrian walkway with wide steps. As we turn in, the remaining six motorcyclists fly past us as we begin a bumpy ride down the steps. The car is beginning to fall apart.

THE PURSUERS DO NOT TAKE LONG to catch up with us. We continue racing down the steps, and with heads almost bouncing off the car roof, it is impossible to make a clear shot.

Charles is in the zone as he keeps us from crashing against the side of the walls. The bikers are on top of us now and they are not able to fire at us either. It is a cat and mouse chase for now. Four of them ride along the side of us and begin smashing into us.

Eventually, we reach the bottom of the steps and drive along a walkway. Luckily there are no people in our path.

Charles shouts at us to hold on tight and yanks the handbrake up as he turns the steering wheel. Two motorbikes slam into the side of us and flip over the car and crash to the ground on the other side. Two other bikers get crushed between the front and back of the car against the wall. Their legs are pinned in and get damaged by the pressure. They try to get their guns out but they are in too much pain. We end up spinning three hundred and sixty degrees before facing forward again. We drive over the two men who flipped over the car. There are only two of them left now.

We are reaching the end of the walkway which has metal posts in the ground to prevent cars from coming through. There are a few objects on the ground along the side of the wall to the right of us. I lean forward and point at the bollards to Charles, shouting at him to slam on the brakes. But he has other ideas. Charles scares us by driving into the wall at an angle at full throttle.

The front of the car bounces up the wall and before we know it, Charles has us driving on our left side only on two wheels. We coast between the two bollards, barely squeezing through.

Once we make it through, Charles slams on the brakes to cause us to crash down on all four wheels. The two motorbikes only notice the two posts at the last minute and have no time to react. They crash into them and their bodies are impaled on the posts. The three of us stare at them to see if they will stir but they are unconscious, wrapped around the posts.

We now head to the bank, even more determined not to be stopped.

THE NOW BEAT-UP car barely gets us there and Charles finds a parking space next to some wealthy person who has a modern Mercedes. We compare our car to theirs and wonder why Stellar could not have one of those as a pool car.

We get out of the car and as I push my door open, it falls away from its hinges and smashes to the ground. I have the handle in my hand still. Stellar stares at me and rolls her eyes at me like the car is not already broken. Charles tries not to smile as I stupidly try to put the door back on.

A businesswoman and man notice us standing by the crumpled car as they walk past. They turn their noses up at us and scurry away like we are in the wrong neighbourhood.

THE OUTSIDE of the bank has arched walls running around the building and you have to walk under them to get to the entrance. The building is made out of sandstone.

When we go inside, the floor is made out of beige marble. The ground floor has tellers, stand-alone enquiry stands and stations to complete cheques and cash deposits. Above the tellers is another floor with offices, desks and administration staff.

It is only us inside and the bank feels like it should be closed.

The three of us walk up to a man behind the enquiry stand and ask to speak to someone about requesting customer bank accounts. We assume he will ask for the bank manager.

The man picks up the phone on his stand to call for someone to come down and assist us. He speaks in his own language so we have no idea what he is saying. Once the call is over, he tells us that someone is coming down.

A few moments later, a very fair Cuban man greets us. He is clean-shaven with short straight dark brown hair. He is slim and tall, wearing heavy-framed glasses.

He introduces himself as Mr Fredrick and walks us upstairs.

.   .   .

HE TAKES us to his desk and enquires what our interest is in finding accounts. Stellar and I take a seat in front of his desk and Charles takes a chair from another desk. Charles sits in between us and we take out our credentials to show to Mr Fredrick.

Mr Fredrick presumes that we are interested in accounts relating to small criminals by giving us a list of accounts that could be suspicious.

Charles stops him in his tracks and specifically asks for a particular list. I remember one of the names when back in Switzerland. I mention the name and we see Mr Fredrick go jittery which tells us that he knows who they are. Anyone else would blindly retrieve what we are asking for.

Mr Fedrick stutters, 'Why would you be interested in Mr Hahn? He is a reputable customer.'

Charles leans forward. 'And every name associated with Mr Hahn, in particular, The Order. And can you lend us your computer?'

He begrudgingly allows us to take over his computer. I call Barney to prepare to upload the electronic version of the bank statements. I ask Barney to convert the files to Excel so Charles and I can manipulate the descriptions and figures. It takes seconds for him to access the accounts with Mr Frederick's assistance.

Charles and Stellar walk around expecting trouble again while I am at the computer standing next to Mr Fredrick. Barney is finding this process a lot easier as, since Switzerland, he has written a program to manage the upload much smoother and faster.


IT TAKES ABOUT twenty minutes to transfer copies onto our servers back in London. We are more or less ready to go now. The Order must have assumed that they would have taken care of us en route. There is no sign of any potential threat.

Finally, the transfer is complete. Charles and Stellar are ready to go and waiting for me. I wait to get off the phone to Barney, thanking him once again.


OUTSIDE, two black Jeeps drive into the car park screeching their tyres and abruptly stopping. They have had short notice to go after them and which bank to head to. They have no idea what their description is but there are three of them. They have been told that there will only be staff and the three of them.

Six men come out of the vehicles and stroll into the bank with their automatic rifles poised. They walk in cautiously, not leaving anything to chance.

The staff behind the teller notice them and know to crouch to the floor behind the counter and stay there.

THE THREE OF us go to casually walk towards the stairs to leave the bank and finally head home. We plan to get the next available flight.

Stellar will fly back to America from here at the same time as us. Charles and I will forward a copy of the intel we gathered on the names and accounts. We go to see about finding a taxi to head back to the hotel to check out.

As we reach the top of the stairs, we hear the sound of loud tapping on the floor near us. Charles sees a small round black object and is curious as to where it fell from. A few seconds later we quickly realise it is an explosive.

Charles shouts out loud, 'Bomb! Move it.'

We bolt to the back of the office and, before we have time to reach the back, there is a huge kaboom. We are lifted off our feet and crash back to the ground.

As the floor fills with smoke, flames and scattered parts, Charles takes a few of our own bombs. He throws three over independently, one after the other. Just like in Switzerland, a gunman comes running up the stairs. I go to get my gun when Stellar, already prepared, fires a round off and makes a clean shoot. I watch the man roll down the stairs.

Three bangs go off simultaneously and we hear screams of pain. Charles takes the lead to get us out of here. There is now a fire filling up the stairs which must be from our bombs. Our only way out is by climbing down from the balcony. Stellar reminds us of the black bags that are line bean bags. Charles hands them out and we throw them over the railing to the ground floor. A few seconds after they hit the floor, they blow up and expand within seconds. We realise they are equivalent to stunt airbags. We jump together to land on the inflatable bags and slowly disperse air after we land on them to cushion our fall.

We quickly assess the area for any more gunmen. They all appear to be dead. We leave straightaway.

# 18

# THE ACCUSED

We had no trouble on the way back to the hotel. I cannot believe that it is over now and we can finally go home. I can finally provide evidence that Mary will believe and have to take up.

Now, we will have to find out who this person is that is feeding information back to The Order. For the life of me, I have no idea who it could be. No one comes across with an axe to grind or criticising The Agency. It is another conversation to have with Miles and for him to take it up with Mary. In the meantime, Mary has already had me bring up The Order a few times.

WE ARE ready to leave the hotel and head for the airport together. We have managed to book our flights to London and Los Angeles. We arrive at the airport a little after five o'clock in the evening.

WE ARE SAT at one of the bars near duty-free. We each have our boarding pass, with Charles and me boarding our flight half an hour before Stellar.

We hear our flight number over the tannoy and say our goodbyes. We hug Stellar in turn and thank her for all her help and accessories. She says to think nothing of it and that she was glad to be asked to tag along. I assure her that we will file copies to her for D.I.A.M.O.N.D.S to follow leads themselves so we can work together.

Stellar wants to stay in touch with us and be kept in the loop and vice versa. She asks if we will try to find the mole in our office. After today, we tell her that we will definitely investigate and find the person, and also, have them arrested.

With that, we leave Stellar at the bar and we slowly walk away to catch our flight. We will be leaving at nine o'clock on a ten-hour flight.

WE LAND in London just before three o'clock in the morning. When it is a sensible time, we will contact Miles to let him know that we are back in England. We are going to have a rest today and be in the office first thing tomorrow. We have not told him about the traitor among us. We will tell him in person.

WHEN WE GET BACK TO CHARLES' apartment, we have a shower and then flake out on his bed. We lie in bed huddled together. We have our thoughts on finally having reliable evidence to back up Ivor's story all those years ago.

We are exhausted but wide awake, not being able to sleep. I stare up at the ceiling with Charles and ponder on the last few days. We are enjoying the comfortable silence.

While having my head filled with all that has gone on, I realise that we are to get an engagement ring. I have a lightbulb moment and turn to Charles to discuss how soon we can get formally engaged. Like me, he begins to get excited and our thoughts turn to wedding bells and a honeymoon. He is keen to buy the ring tomorrow. We are going to find a ring during our lunch hour.

It would have been nice for Charles to ask my dad for his permission. I think my dad would have been proud to have Charles as a son-in-law.

After a couple of hours of discussing what type I ring I would like, we eventually drift off into a deep sleep.

BARNEY HAS COME into the office before five o'clock in the morning to finalise his PowerPoint presentation. With the help of the bank accounts and crypto transactions, he makes his case. He is adding relevant cost descriptions to support his theory of The Order having a horrifying plan. He is going to have Stephanie look over his slides with a fresh pair of eyes, to add her own input to make sure it makes sense and does not leave any ambiguity for Mary to find fault with.

Barney is still wondering when it will be a good time to tell Jane about the other thing he discovered, after investigating two men who worked for Vladimir.

Before he realises it, the time is eight o'clock and people are coming to work. He sees Stephanie coming from the lift and he gets her attention. Stephanie notices Barney waving at her to come over.

THEY AGREE to meet at lunchtime to discuss his presentation. Stephanie suggests showing his work on a tablet so it is less conspicuous. Barney prefers to discuss it outside the office. They arrange to meet on the corner of Glasshouse Walk, a five-minute walk away. They will leave the office separately and meet at one o'clock.

I GET into the office with Charles close to ten o'clock and go straight to Barney's desk to discuss having access to The Order's accounts.

Barney notices us and begins to be fidgety. 'So, you have come to get a copy of the names and transactions I extracted?'

I feel anxious and excited to have a hold of the data, 'Yep. Is it on a USB or hard drive?'

Barney smiles and shakes his head, 'I don't think so. I have created a password access to the server. You will need to use your desktop to see what has been uploaded. The file was too big to store on a USB or external hard drive.'

Charles is not surprised. 'It took ages to wait for you to upload the information. Even I know a USB-size storage would not fit. What's the password?'

Barney writes down the combination of letters and numbers. 'There you go. Everything will be there. It is easier to print the relevant pages.'

We thank him for his work and then head to Miles' office to let him know what we found out.

WE CAN SEE Miles sat behind his desk and he waits for us to come in after we knock. I go in first and take a seat before we give him the details.

Miles asks how the Virgin Islands were; 'Did you make the most of the stay in Charlotte Amalie?'

Charles gives a brief description; 'We saw a little of the place. The people were friendly.'

Miles wants to know how our trip went. 'Was it straightforward getting the information you needed?'

I think back over what we went through. 'We faced hostility. We made a new friend called Stellar Star. She thinks we have a spy amongst us.'

Miles is half-listening until I mention the word 'spy'. 'Why did she think that?'

Charles explains, 'Someone really didn't want us getting the information. The only people who knew where we were going were you and Barney. You're not a mole and neither is Barney. The Order could not have known about our trip without help. Especially with Epstein. No one knew we were going on his island. Apart from you.'

Miles takes a moment to think, 'Why not Stellar tipping them off?'

I vouch for her, 'She helped us escape them in Switzerland. Killed some of them. She came with us to Cuba. Helped us to get the information. Also, she gave us cover when we were in the Virgin Islands.'

Miles is curious as to why she appeared. 'Who is this girl Stellar? Who does she work for?'

I tell him what she told us, 'She works for an unknown private agency called D.I.A.M.O.N.D.S.'

Miles has a blank expression. 'What is that short for?'

I think back to what she said the acronym stood for; "Defence In All Manner Of National and Domestic Security'.'

Miles has not heard of them before but is happy. 'Right. So, we have a spy in our organisation. How do we find this person?'

Charles has an idea, 'Stellar said that her people had a mole. They created a fictitious breakthrough with a piece of new information. They put it on a secure server. Only one person had access to the server. They caught the person hacking it. So, we do the same. We only use one server and only one person gets access. We monitor the server. When the mole hacks in, we use their digital print to lead us to them.'

Miles is impressed. 'Do it. Barney will be the single user.'

Charles brings up the subject of his friend. 'Did you give your friend Gordon closure?'

Miles adjusts his mannerism; 'Yeah. He was relieved that the person responsible was taken care of. I didn't tell him that it wasn't you.'

I can see that Gordon is more than a friend, so I add, 'We made sure he paid before he was killed.'

We finish the briefing and go back to Barney to set up a trap.


WE STAND in front of his desk and quietly ask him to follow us to another room. Barney can see that there is a reason. He can see that we have an idea.

The three of us leave the floor and take the lift to the ground floor. We go to one of the leather sofas they have in the lobby area.

Barney is sarcastic, 'I assume it isn't to do with the password not working.'

I ignore his comment. 'We need you to create a fake message that we know more information on The Order. Put it on a separate stand-alone server. Only you have access to it.'

Barney is puzzled as to why; 'What is going on?'

Charles explains, 'We believe that we have someone feeding information back to The Order. They seemed to know where we were every time.'

Barney is shocked; 'We have a spy?'

I ask him to pay attention; 'We need you to set this up as soon as you can.'

Barney stares at both of us alternately, 'Do you have a clue to who it could be?'

Charles tells him that we do not have anyone in mind. 'Can you do this today?'

Barney says that it is not a problem but he will have to do this after lunch. We only care that it can be set up anytime today.

Once we have Barney on board, we go back upstairs and ask Barney not to mention this to anyone. He knows the gravity of the situation and will be discrete.


CHARLES and I go to our desks and begin analysing the data we retrieved in Switzerland first to see what they have been buying on the dark web. We think that the bank accounts in Cuba will be transfers between the two platforms.

We are aiming to interpret the acquisitions to see what long-term goals they have for their agenda. While we sift through the multiple lines of descriptions and figures, I cannot stop thinking about buying the engagement ring. I keep clock-watching for when it is lunchtime. I wonder if Charles is thinking the same while I watch him, deep in thought, trawling the data on the computer screen.

I keep staring at him to see if he notices me doing it. He seems to be in his own world and not realising that I am staring at him.

I find myself losing focus and think I will get into this once I have the ring on my finger. Right now, I cannot focus. My eyes are going blurry.

Eventually, it is midday and I make a point of letting Charles know, and bluntly, about the mission of finding a ring today.

Charles is now keen to get out of the office as well and already knows which shop to go to.


BARNEY HAS ALSO BEEN FEELING the time dragging as he is keen to meet up with Stephanie to show her his findings. He wants to show Mary later in the afternoon after office hours so there is no interruption with work.

. . .

WE WALK AWAY from Vauxhall Bridge along the same road to a jewellery shop that he knows. He seems to only want to go to one particular place. I hoped that we would go to a few to savour the experience.

We walk for about ten minutes and take a right turn down a quiet road. He takes me to 'Coleman Douglas Pearls', an independent store. He has me curious now and I wait for him to unveil his secrecy.

WE WALK into the shop and see a woman behind the counter. She smiles at us as if she was expecting us. She points her finger up as if to say one moment. She goes out back while we wait next to the glass counter. I peer into the counter observing the trinkets and necklaces displayed under clinical lighting. I wonder about buying something from here before we leave. I still have not spent any of my inheritance money yet. I want to keep it there so I have some kind of tangible memory of my parents.

The woman returns with a box that you would find a ring inside. It is covered in a navy-blue fabric and she passes to Charles. I wonder why we are not discussing what kind of ring we are looking for.

Before I realise what I think is happening, Charles goes on one knee and opens the lid to reveal a diamond ring. I am stunned as I assumed that we would be picking it together.

Charles shows no expression on his face, 'Will you do me the honour of being my wife?'

I have knots in my stomach as I realise he has already chosen the ring. I cannot speak as I frantically gesture with my hands to my cheeks. Charles cannot see whether it is a yes or a no and asks me.

It takes me a while to blurt out the words, 'Yes. Of course, yes.'

Charles stands up and takes the ring out of the box as his hands shake. He nervously slides the ring onto my finger. My hand begins to shake as the realisation sinks in.

I cannot help getting emotional as I think about my parents, wishing that they were here. I know they would want to see their last child getting engaged.

ON OUR WAY back to the office, I cannot help holding my hand out in the light to see the diamonds glisten. I want to let my siblings know but Charles wants family to know later. He is only interested in us and not people knowing. Already, I want to set a date for next year and plan the wedding now.

Charles will leave it all to me and let me lead the whole process. I almost trip over a loose paving slab as I gaze at the way the diamonds are shaped into a square.

. . .

WE ARE HALFWAY to the office when we see Barney standing at the side of the road. He is a few yards in front of us. I want Barney to be one of the first to know about our engagement. Charles sighs and begrudgingly allows me to catch up with him and show off the ring. He is happy to let me walk on ahead.

I wave at Barney to get his attention but he seems to be deep in thought and withdrawn. I sense he has something on his mind as he does not notice me.

I stop walking and begin being more theatrical trying to get his attention. Charles catches up with me and sees what is going on.

Charles senses something is not quite right. 'Jane. Stop what you doing. Something is not right. Just hang back.'

I do not sense anything is wrong, 'He is probably waiting for a taxi. Leaving early from work.'

Charles knows Barney's quirks, 'He is not going home. He has to do that task we asked of him. He is waiting for someone.'

I wonder who it could be. 'He never told us he was going to see someone. It must be his girlfriend.'

Charles suggests we hold back and wait to see who it is.


WE SEE a black transit van screech in front of Barney and hear the side door slide open. Barney is stunned and we can see this is not a part of his meeting.

Someone with black sleeves grapples him and pulls him inside the back of the van. We bolt after the van to try to stop them from driving away, but we are not fast enough to reach them in time.

The van zooms off, revving the engine. Charles tries to stop a vehicle in the road so we can confiscate it. The drivers are speeding up rather than slowing down.

A motorbike comes up the road and to ensure the rider stops, he kicks his leg in the air at his chest. The motorcyclist flips off the back and the motorbike collapses and crashes into a bollard. He then quickly grabs the bike and shouts at me to get on the back.

We then go after the van.


THEY ARE NOT in sight and we hope that we have not lost the van. Charles is moving through the gears like flicking a switch. I never knew he could ride a motorbike. I grab hold of his waist as tight as possible and hope we do not crash. We are not wearing helmets.

The wind is rushing against our faces like an air tunnel as we travel at sixty miles an hour. It feels a lot faster than in the car.

We are still no closer to seeing the van and I wonder if it turned off onto a side street. As I give up all hope, Charles shouts out that the van is up ahead. I see it myself and have hope that we can catch up with them.

We weave in between the traffic with a couple of drivers sounding their horns. We jump traffic lights almost mowing down crossing pedestrians. We almost career into a London bus as it pulls out from the bus stop but Charles anticipates the driver.

As we approach the van, the back doors fling open and they fire on us.

# 19

## ALMOST

Charles heads for the pavement when there is a gap in the stationary cars. We use the parked cars for cover as they try to hit us.

We hear the windows of the vehicles smash as we pass them. A few shards of glass merely miss us. It does not deter us from saving Barney.

I wonder why these people would want to kidnap Barney. It is not like he can be used as an exchange for us. Barney is not a bargaining chip except that he is a close friend.

The van takes the next left and there is not enough room for us to use the pavement to take a left. We get back on the road in time to take a sharp turn into the road. They stop firing at us but we keep a distance in case. We can see that the road is reaching a junction and the van screeches left. It would appear that they are heading back towards the Thames. As soon as the van is out of sight, Charles accelerates rapidly so we do not lose them. I think we are not going to make the corner and fly into a parked car. Charles leans left so we are almost horizontal as we make a hard left and then straighten up.

We then see the van approaching another junction at the end of the road. It makes a sharp left again. A few seconds later, we make the same turn and then see the van turn sharp right. As we approach the right junction, a car comes out of a left junction and Charles has to slam on the brakes. We almost slam into the car sideways. The driver is petrified, with his white knuckles grasping the steering wheel. I nervously smile before Charles revs the engine and drops the clutch. We zoom off, closing the gap between us and them. They begin to fire at us again and we zig-zag to avoid being hit. I wish I had my gun but we did not expect to face trouble when picking up an engagement ring.

Eventually, the van slams on its brakes when it reaches the Thames. The driver and two men with Barney come out of the van and run towards the river.

We stop behind the van and run in their direction towards the water. When we reach the edge, we see them riding off in a speedboat.

THERE IS a boat gently moving in the water and appears to be mooring up near us. We take this opportunity to steal it.

We jump onto the pontoon instead of taking the steps. Then, we jump onto the boat as it docks. We shout at the occupants to get off. We introduce ourselves as secret service and flash our identification.

Then we commandeer the speedboat. Charles yanks the throttle back and the engine roars as we take off.

It is not long before we catch up with them and ride alongside them. They begin to shoot at us as their boat crashes through the water. We ram into the side of them before they have a chance to fire off a round.

I can see Barney is stressed by the ordeal as he is showing he is scared. We try to get close to them so we can have Barney come onto our boat.

Just when we think we can retrieve him, we approach a tall sea buoy and have to swerve in time to avoid hitting it.

We make another attempt as we move to the side of them. When we are almost touching, I make an attempt to grab him. One of the men pulls Barney away from my grasp. Then another man slams his fist into my face. I go flying backwards and land on my back. My nose instantly flows blood. I use my sleeve to wipe the blood. Charles checks to see if I am okay.

As I struggle to get onto my feet because of the rocking of the boat, I notice a helicopter flying overhead. It is heading towards the OXO Tower. I have a sickening feeling that they are going to try to take Barney in it. I go to try again to grab Barney but one of them grabs me and tries to drag me onto their boat.

Charles grabs the end of my trouser leg to stop me from falling into their boat. The man then throws punches in the side of my stomach until I let go of Barney. I slide away and crumple inside our boat in pain. I feel like my ribs are broken after that onslaught.

I fight through the pain and force myself up. As I get to my feet, I notice that we are heading towards the edge of the Thames. The other boat begins to slow down and Charles does the same.

Neither boat slows down fast enough and they slam against the bank of the Thames. The side of the boat disintegrates with splinters of white fibreglass. The other boat is in a similar condition.

Charles and I are knocked off our feet towards the back of the boat. I land on my right side, the one that received those punches. Pain shoots through my abdomen which causes me to scream. Charles scrambles towards me to see that I am okay. As he reaches me, we hear more gunfire and Charles covers me. The onslaught of bullets eventually stops. Charles stares me in the eyes to see if I am okay. We forget where we are for a second and we briefly kiss.

THE THREE MEN hustle Barney off the sinking boat and head to the OXO Tower through the maintenance door. They take the rickety cage lift to the top floor where they are getting picked up by a helicopter.

Barney has no idea why they have kidnapped him. He is too worried to try and fight them off him.

WE SEE the four of them walk through the metal door of the building. We notice water seeping into the boat now, ankle-deep. We wade through the water and run up the stone steps to the tower.

The lift is already going up. Our only option is the stairs.

I thought the lift would be quick but it is creaking as it travels up like a snail. We are out-running them which will give us a chance to meet them at the top. The three men try to deter us by firing again. I wish we carried our guns even though they are only used for field trips. We drop to the steps to avoid being hit. I forget about how much my side aches until I slam into the rusty mesh steps. It does not slow us down and we are still ahead of them.

We reach the top with about a minute to spare before the lift catches up with us.

CHARLES and I wonder what we are going to do when they arrive at the top. We try to find any objects that we can use as weapons. I see a long slim metal strip and decide to use that. There is nothing else and so Charles will use his skills to disarm them himself.

We go through a hatch in the ceiling that takes us onto the roof. We wait for a few seconds before they begin to come through. Without warning, bullets come through the roof near us and we roll away. The shooting stops and we grapple back into position.

We see one of the men's black sleeves coming out of the hole with a gun and I swipe his wrist. The gun flies out of his hand and Charles goes for it. Another person tries to climb out onto the roof. They do not have their guns out as they try to clamber out. I whack his fingers clasping to the edge of the square hole. The hand quickly releases, then another hand comes out and grabs my arm. I try to wriggle myself free of his grasp but their grip is too strong. I end up getting pulled towards them. The man comes out and I feel his fist plough into my face till I almost pass out. The man shoves me aside.

CHARLES SEES me lying near the hatch which makes him angry. He waits for them to come out, letting them think that they are safe. When he has a clear shot, he takes it and kills one of them instantly. The other two come out firing at Charles. He dives and rolls to avoid being hit.

This gives the two men, keeping a hold on Barney, a chance to run for the helicopter hovering above the roof.

Charles sees the helicopter descending to allow the three of them to get on board. He glances at Jane to see how she is before turning to the pilot to disable him and stop them from flying away. As he fires, one of them turns round and fires more rounds in his direction. Charles rolls along the roof again to avoid the bullets. He misjudges the edge of the roof and almost falls off. He slides the gun along the roof so he has both hands free. His fingers grasp the ledge and gradually, he pulls himself up. He manages to get his elbows onto the edge and then pull himself up.

He then quickly gets himself fully back on the roof and grabs the gun to try and stop them from getting away.

I HEAR the commotion and glance up to see if Charles is harmed. I see the helicopter flying away with Barney and the kidnappers inside. I notice there is a fourth man inside who is dressed in a suit. I wonder how the fourth man changed into a suit at the last minute. Then I notice there is a dead man by the hatch and realise that the fourth man was already inside the helicopter.

From what I could see, the man was old with some grey hair and bald on top.

I see Charles running up the edge of the roof and then emptying the gun until he has no more bullets left. The helicopter is long gone with Barney in it.

I begin to get emotional as Barney is like a brother to me and Charles is deflated with his head bowed down and his arms by his side.

BARNEY SEES a man sat opposite him who he knows straight away. He is on his crazy wall. The man introduces himself as Xavier Hark.

Xavier gives him an evil smile and says, 'I need you to fix a problem.'

Barney is dubious of his request. 'What makes you think I will help you?'

Xavier uses a threat, 'I know you have a girlfriend called Kate. You live in Brixton. I got to you. I can get to her anytime. Is that good enough as a threat?'

Barney believes him. 'So, what is it you want me to do?'

Xavier stares out of the window. 'We have a glitch. A code that needs fixing. I understand you are a whizz at writing code. If you are working for The Agency, you can work for us.'

Barney is puzzled; 'How did you know I was going to be waiting there?'

Xavier is vague; 'We just had to find the right time. You were going for lunch?'

Barney does not mention his meeting, 'Yeah. I was crossing the road when your goons came.'

There is no more conversation as the helicopter rides away from London.

# 20

# FALSELY ACCUSED

We are back at The Agency in Miles' office giving him a briefing of what we experienced. Miles is shocked to hear what happened and cannot understand why. We have no idea ourselves and cannot come up with a reason.

Miles has to sit down as he tries to figure out what Barney would have done to be a threat. I suggest that it could be related to The Order clutching at straws. I cannot think of any other assignments that would cause him to be kidnapped.

Charles is tracing back over what Barney could have been working on that could have upset someone. He is struggling to think of a reason himself.

Miles suggests we go through his computer and work schedule to see if anything comes up. I suggest we get someone from another IT department to find the answer faster. He will have passwords that are tough to crack. Charles agrees with me.

Miles gives me a funny stare. 'You should go home. Clean yourself up.'

I notice my sleeve is smothered in blood and take his advice. As I go to walk out, he notices my ring. I play it down as a present to myself but Miles whistles when he sees how much it gleams. Charles does not say anything as he is deep in thought figuring out who

As I go to walk out of his office, I see Rupert Jones.

RUPERT IS Caucasian in his mid-fifties. He is tall and slim, standing at six foot six inches. He has an oval-shaped head with a narrow, pointed nose.

He has black hair that is thinning on top with thick hair on the sides and back. He talks with a posh voice.

He wears three-piece suits and a long wool overcoat with black shiny shoes.

He went to Oxford University and joined MI6 after graduation. When Mary was killed, Rupert became her successor.

Charles has history with Rupert because he tried to make a pass at his wife when she was alive. They were colleagues when Charles was working at MI6 but never worked together. The last time they saw each other, Charles punched him for making a pass at me. That was a couple of years ago.

RUPERT IS NOT HAPPY; in fact, he is angry. I wonder what Miles has done to upset him now. He is with two other men in dark corporate suits.

Before I realise what is about to happen, the two men grip my arms and hold them back. I wince as they are rough with me.

I see a brown foolscap clutched in Rupert's hand and I'm not sure what is going on.

Miles comes out of his office and immediate barks at Rupert, 'What is this about? Why are you arresting Jane?'

Rupert waves the folder in his hand, 'I have it on good authority that Jane Knight has been trading on the black market on the dark web. She has been buying and selling arms over the last four years.'

Miles finds the accusation absurd. 'That is absolute bull. Where did you get the information from?'

Rupert is sticking by his accusation. 'An unknown source sent this into our office. We found it at the reception desk. There is a paper trail a mile long showing payments and receipts with Jane's name all over them. Do you know how serious this is?'

Miles sighs, 'I know. Treason. But you better be sure you want to go down this path.'

I think about what Epson said, 'Son of a bit...'

Charles launches at Rupert by his collar and drags him against the glass wall of Miles' office, 'This is a set up by The Order. We traced an Epson Bernstein and he told us that he organised the whole thing.'

Rupert shrugs off his grip. 'Then Jane has nothing to worry about. We will get him to confess.'

Charles remembers that he is dead now and says, 'Well, that is a problem. He is filled with lead. He made the wrong investment.'

Rupert pushes Charles back and straightens his tie and suit. 'That is convenient. I cannot ignore this. Jane is smart and has the know-how with her knowledge and experience.'

Miles pushes the two men away from Jane. 'Take the cuffs off. Jane told me about Epstein creating false transactions on behalf of The Order. This was when they were in the Virgin Islands. Since then, we have found their bank accounts and blockchain ledger that happens to be on the dark web. This is pretty convenient when we have The Order banged to rights.'

I have no idea if they are going to arrest me or take the handcuffs off. While I watch them bicker amongst themselves, I see Mary walk over from the lift.

Mary came here to discuss Barney's kidnap. 'What is going on here? I came here to discuss the disappearance of one of our colleagues. Why is Jane being accused of his kidnapping?'

Miles briefs her, 'Jane is being accused of funding terrorism.'

Mary chortles. 'You are having a joke, right? Rupert, uncuff Jane. Someone, tell me who started this rumour.'

Rupert passes her the folder he has in his hand. 'This will tell you everything.'

Mary snatches it out of his hand in a huff and peruses the content. 'Hmm. This looks like Mickey Mouse prepared this. These are photocopies. Where are the bank cards associated with the bank account? The bank statements sent to her home address? I assume you went to her apartment to gather passwords, her computer and raided her personal accounts.'

Rupert looks embarrassed. 'Well, we are going to get to that point.'

Mary tuts; 'Well, what are you doing here? Take those handcuffs off. She will be in my custody until you get concrete evidence to back up these flimsy bits of paper. Just like how Jane and Charles gather their intel, you do the same.'

Rupert begrudgingly tells his men to take the cuffs off. He accepts Mary taking responsibility for Jane. Then she orders him and his men to leave her floor at once. She barks at Miles, Charles and myself to go into Miles' office.


MARY IS VEXED, using curse words I never thought would leave her lips. 'Now that I have got that out of my system, talk to me. Not you. Charles.'

Charles composes his thoughts; 'We saw Epson. He told us about working for The Order. He said that he created real accounts to frame Jane to discredit her reputation so that you and Miles would not believe her about them. He gave us the lead to Switzerland. From there, Barney discovered that the accounts lead back to Cuba. And now we believe The Order have Barney. But we don't know why.'

Mary stands there letting it all sink in. 'Right. Now, where is the data?'

I intervene, 'On our servers. It was too big to have on a separate hard drive or USB stick. With a password.'

Mary continues to digest the information; 'Could Barney have been kidnapped for stealing their information?'

Miles forms his own opinion. 'Yes. But we have another problem. We have a spy in our organisation. We had a plan to plant a fake piece of evidence on a stand-alone server and only have Barney access the server. Then, we would wait for the mole to go for the bait. But now he is not here, that is out the window.'

Mary is shocked. 'How did you come by this?'

I tell her about Stellar. 'We met a new ally. She suggested we had a spy because it happened to her organisation. The man she tracked down said they are placed in many intelligence offices.'

Mary is dubious. 'Why believe her?'

Charles brings up coincidences; 'We had people try to kill us in Switzerland and Cuba. The only people who knew of our itinerary were Barney and Miles. It was also strange when we had our second assignment. They knew we were at Jane's sister's house; then also in Florida. Chae was working for them.'

Mary finds our theory more plausible. 'And now Barney is kidnapped. It cannot be a coincidence. Do we have a suspect?'

Miles answers, 'No.'

Mary thinks for a while, then she says, 'Give me time to come up with a plan. Charles, you continue analysing the data on The Order. You and Jane believed that they have a plan. If they do, we will find it in their financial records. Especially if they tried to kill you for it. Jane will be with me. Miles, figure out a way to bring our foe out into the open. We need to interrogate them on what they know about involvement in The Order. Jane, I guess you finally have our attention. I'm sorry it has taken this long to prove your belief.'

I appreciate her apology; 'Thank you.'

WITH THAT, I gather my things from my desk and then go with Mary to be baby-sat. I ask if I can go home to freshen up first but she glares at me. I take that as a 'no' and she treats me like a daughter as she moans at me to hurry up.

I notice Charles and mouth to him that I love him before scurrying off after Mary. Charles smiles at me and gestures reassurance.

MARY and I walk through the exit barrier at reception. As we walk out, I notice a maintenance man who brushes past me and apologises quietly under his breath. I do not think anything of it and continue following Mary outside of the building where her personal driver is waiting for us.

A MAINTENANCE MAN wearing a light blue boiler suit is wearing a worn cap matching his overall. He is young, in his early thirties, and wearing a moustache. He is carrying an old beige rucksack. He comes out of the lift and turns left to walk towards the server room.

He is suspicious but none of the staff takes notice of him as he casually strolls to the room. He has a work visitor's badge to avoid suspicion. He discretely takes out a piece of cardboard with a handwritten floor plan to find out where the room is.

When he reaches the door, he takes out a lockpick to open the door. He checks to see if anyone is watching him before he goes inside.

Once inside, he is overwhelmed by how many servers are in the room and is not sure which server will house The Order's bank account details.

He has enough explosives with him in case this would happen. Instead of trying the find the relevant server, he begins placing them next to every fifth machine.

While he is placing explosives, he hears voices and thinks someone is going to come in. He quickly hides in case they come in and checks that his knife is easily to hand.

The indistinct chatter fades away and he finishes placing his bombs.

When he has completed his task, he quickly leaves the room and walks back to the lift.

CHARLES IS ALREADY at his desk, going through the files on the server. He keeps staring at Jane's empty chair, wishing that Jane were here helping him. As he leans back in his chair and puts his hands behind his head, Charles becomes overwhelmed with where to begin analysing the data. As he ponders on the mammoth task, something catches his eye.

He notices a maintenance man appearing suspicious as he watches him glancing over his shoulder nervously. He also sees him being anxious waiting for the lift to arrive. When the man gets in the lift, he goes for a stroll to see where he has been.

Charles stands up and walks over in the direction the maintenance man came from. He wonders what he could have been servicing. There is not much there apart from a corridor and the server room.

He stares at the server room thinking that he might have gone in there. He senses that something is not right and feels compelled to take a wander. He peers through the glass wall and looks inside to see if anything appears out of place. Considering how his day has been, he tries the door knowing it should be locked and someone should have let him in.

The door opens, which is not good, and he goes in straight away. He tries to find anything out of place. As he walks through the room amongst the servers, he trips over something on the floor. Charles assumes he has lifted up a loose bit of carpet as he goes to put it back. When he does, he notices that he tripped over a small plastic box. He bends down to study the out-of-place box. He soon realises what it is.

# 21

# CASUALTY OF WAR

I wonder where Mary is taking me as she has not told me our destination. We are driving over Vauxhall Bridge at the moment. We are sat in the back of a black Jaguar car. I see the glass partition slide up.

Mary waits for the glass to fully close before turning to me. 'I need you outside here and not locked up. You have believed in this conspiracy from day one and finally found concrete evidence.'

I wonder what I can do without The Agency's resources, so I ask, 'How can I help on my own?'

Mary is not fazed by my situation. 'Find your original whistle-blower, Ivor Peteski. Tell him what you know and what information he can give and feed it back to us.'

I do not think that he will have anything new; 'I have not heard from Ivor in three years. He is not in the loop with them.'

Mary is not interested. 'Go home. Pack what you need. Then contact Ivor. Get him to meet you somewhere. Then go underground and, between you two, find out what the threat is and where they have taken Barney to.'

I think of worse case scenario. 'What if I cannot locate him?'

Mary has a solution; 'Contact Charles and use him to locate him if you cannot.'

I guess she has thought of everything. 'What if my passport is flagged up as a risk?'

Mary reassures me that I will make it out of the country. 'Trust me, you will.'

I consider a way of making contact; 'Do I call you on your landline or mobile?'

Mary thinks for a moment, 'Stay in contact with Charles and he will relay back to me.'

I have a thought; 'Rupert will have forensics at my apartment.'

Mary has thought about that already and says, 'They need a warrant. They are not a law within themselves. They will not be there now.'

We finish our conversation and Mary asks the driver to take me to the nearest tube station to head home.

WITH THE HELP OF MILES, Charles has already asked staff to leave the floor. Staff leave in an orderly fashion using the fire exit stairs.

Miles and Charles have already arranged a bomb squad to try to rectify the situation through damage control.

While waiting, they keep themselves outside the room in case they activate the devices and have space to run for cover.

They have no idea how much destruction the bombs will cause, or how many have been laid down. It has been over ten minutes since calling the bomb squad.

The room begins to light up with small L.E.D lights coming from each explosive. They know what this means and begin running to the other side of the office. Halfway across the open-plan office, the bombs are detonated and there is a huge explosion.

The force rips a hole in the external wall at the back of the server room. Clumps of rubble and dust fall to the ground within the vicinity of the grounds. A few cars are parked below and they get completed destroyed by the loose debris. Car alarms are set off.

Charles and Miles are covered in dust and avoid being trapped under rubble. They can see that the force of the explosion has ripped a hole in the floor and they can see the floor below.

Charles and Miles cough from the fine dust entering their lungs. Jane pops into Charles' mind and wonders about her safety. He tells Miles that he is going after Jane. He accepts his priority and tells him to go.

A MOTORBIKE IS RIDING towards Mary's car and the cyclist is holding a magnetic bomb in the palm of his hand. He rides up to the car, overtaking traffic at a safe distance so as not to attract attention to himself. As the rider gets close, he leans down on the left side of the bike and aims to stick the bomb near the petrol tank.

The cyclist quietly sticks it on the petrol cap without slowing down and then zooms off. The explosive is on a timer and will go off in two minutes.

.   .   .

THE DRIVER REACHES Pimlico underground station. Her driver stops on the side of the road for me to get out.

I WATCH Mary being driven off before I go inside the tube station. As I turn to walk away, I hear a massive explosion. The ground shakes like an earthquake and causes me to lose my footing. The shockwaves shatter car windows and nearby shopfront windows.

I quickly get to my feet and search for Mary's car, hoping that she has already driven clear away. However, I cannot see anything with the thick dark grey smoke billowing from ground zero. I soon notice it is coming from Mary's car.

I run over to the burning wreck thinking that I will see her and the driver alive. I can only get within ten feet because of the heat and the smoke. There is no way that either survived. I wonder if that bomb was meant for me as I have been accused of embezzlement. But why would someone frame me for fraud then try to kill me? She must have been getting close to the existence of The Order herself.

I do not stay around for the police and head home straight away.

WHEN I GET to my apartment building, my hand shakes when I use the key to open my door. My neighbour, Steve, from across the way notices me and walks over to make conservation. He notices my sleeve covered in blood and shows concern. I lie and explain that it is not mine and someone had an accident at work. He tries to pry into what happened but I am not in the mood. I tell him that I need the bathroom and really need to go quickly.

He still continues the conversation as I close the door on him and his voice muffles.

I FRANTICALLY CALL Charles to hear his voice and let him know what has happened. 'Ah, I am glad to hear your voice. Mary is dead! Mary is dead!'

Charles shouts at me to calm down, 'I know. The police informed us. They also blew up the server and destroyed the data we retrieved. It ripped a hole in the ground and the outside wall. I am on my way to you. Where are you now?'

I cannot believe what he has told me. 'I'm at home. Come and get me.'

Charles shouts down the phone, 'Hold tight. I'm on my way.'

I can hear motor vehicle horns blowing and screeching tyres. 'Please hurry.'

·   ·   ·

CHARLES IS RACING along with blue sirens flashing through the front grill of a black Ford saloon car. He overtakes slow traffic on the other side of the road at traffic islands, flashing his headlights at on-coming cars to slow down. He almost crashes into the side of red buses as he squeezes in between them and on-coming cars. A couple of pedestrians trying to cross the road at traffic lights or islands are almost mown down.

Charles has been racing to Jane's apartment for the past twenty-five minutes with another ten minutes to go. He is anxious to have her in his arms after witnessing their main boss being killed in an explosion. He is like a devil possessed as he leaves carnage behind him as cars, motorcyclists, as well as taxis and buses, all swerve to avoid him.

He takes calculated risks driving through traffic lights that are directing traffic.

I HOLD my hand out in front of me and still find my hands are shaking. The doorbell goes and causes me to jump. I do not want to answer it thinking it could be a threat. I speak out asking who is it. It is Steve again wanting to check if I'm okay. I stare out of my window, at Homerton Overground station and sigh as I am not in a mood for conversation. As I turn round to walk to the door to tell him that I am not interested, bullets fly into my apartment from outside, ripping through my walls. I dive to the ground and crawl into a foetal position and close my ears.

The sound of a helicopter and the machine gun is unbearably loud, piercing my eardrum. My favourite sofa, only a few years old, gets shredded by the rounds of bullets whizzing through my living room. All I see is white foam floating in the air and fabric debris getting tossed everywhere.

I am hoping Steven is okay as I watch my front door being turned into Swiss cheese. My kitchen is written off now. The only part of my apartment that is intact is my floor.

CHARLES FINALLY ARRIVES at Jane's apartment and can hear the shower of bullets. He thinks the worst and rushes inside up to her floor.

When he reaches her apartment, he can see hundreds of bullet holes in the wall opposite her door. He sees Steven huddled on the floor, frozen. He can see he is in shock and wonders if he will ever say hi to Jane ever again. He runs past Jane's door, in between on-coming bullets to drag Steve up and clear him to safety.

He then runs to her door and lies on the ground feet first. He kicks the door to open it, then suddenly, the door disintegrates before his eyes. He then crawls quickly inside her apartment.

. . .

I FINALLY HEAR CHARLES' voice shouting out my name. He orders me to crawl towards him, so I begin moving towards him. There is a pause that I take advantage of and get out of my apartment into the corridor.

Charles and I hug with relief. Then Charles wants to take out the helicopter. He tells me to stay outside.


CHARLES REACHES the living room and stares at the pilot, only focusing on him. He gets out his gun from his holster and aims at the base of the rotor blades. He aims while blocking out the sounds and vision of the hail of bullets. He counts to five to slow his reactions and focus.

Despite the chaos around him, he keeps calm and makes one shot. The rotor sparks and then malfunctions. The pilot has to fight the controls to keep the helicopter in the air. Charles does not hear an explosion and so assumes it has not crashed, but at least there is no more danger.


I DO NOT HEAR any more gunfire and assume that Charles has taken care of them. He comes back out walking.

Charles is relaxed as he puts away his gun. 'You always did want a remodelling of your apartment. Let's get outta here.'

I stand up and brush myself down; 'I think we are getting closer to them.'

Charles glances at Steve. 'We make sure he is alright then get you out of the country.'


AFTER MAKING sure my neighbour is okay, we drive out of the Homerton area and Charles is quiet about where he is taking me. I do not pry as he knows what he is doing.

A phone call comes in on the car speakers via Bluetooth and we hear Miles' voice; 'Did you get her safely?'

I speak up, 'I'm here. The apartment is trashed but we made it out okay.'

Miles goes quiet. 'What happened to your flat?'

Charles talks, 'They sent a helicopter to take her out. I thought overkill. I'm on our way to the airfield. A plane is waiting there for us.'

Miles sounds relieved on the phone. 'Don't stop for anything. Expect your ETA to be thirty minutes. Ivor is only hanging around for ten minutes. So, don't be late.'

With that, Miles hangs up and I ask Charles how they knew about Mary's plan. Charles smiles and tells me that Mary was to let me know outside the office so no one would know what the plan was. 'We will get the people who killed her and tried to get you. But for now, you go into hiding. Miles told me the plan via a secure line to my mobile. While you were being interrogated.'

Everything makes sense now. 'So, what do I do when I get to my destination?'

Charles says the same as Mary, 'Whoever finds you, we will know the mole. No one knows in the office about this. When the leak takes place, we will be able to hone in on the person.'

I have an idea that I will be the bait. 'I guess that I will be the maggot on the hook.'

Charles does not express comfort as he says, 'Well, I will be keeping tabs on you.'

WE ARRIVE at Farnborough Airport in Hampshire in good time. Ivor is standing outside his plane waiting for us. We get out of the car and I smile at Ivor as he does the same.

Charles has no expression as he goes to shake Ivor's hand. We stand in a triangle briefly. Ivor is keen to leave as he appears distracted. I really do not want to separate from Charles and ask if he wants to come, hoping he will say yes. He stares at me and I can tell that he wants to come with me but he cannot.

Ivor goes inside the plane to allow me to say goodbye to my boyfriend. We face each other and touch with the tips of our fingers. We do not need to say anything as I well up and a tear falls down the side of my cheek. Charles holds my cheeks in the palm of his hands and wipes my tear with his thumb.

HE REMINDS ME THAT, when this is all over, we have something to look forward to which is our official engagement. He is trying to use the thought of officially being engaged and planning our wedding as a light at the end of the tunnel.

We then passionately kiss, making the most of this moment. Our last few minutes of time together makes me French kiss him so I can be as close as possible. We eventually tear ourselves apart and he allows me to go. Before I walk away, he gives me a burner phone to keep in contact and also pulls out a gold necklace. Before I go all mushy, he tells me that it has a tracker inside the heart-shaped locket, so, he can literally keep track of my whereabouts.

I walk backwards up the small steps to the plane not taking my eyes off him. Charles does not move until he can no longer see me.

CHARLES HANGS around till the plane takes off.

IVOR and I make ourselves comfortable as we sit opposite each other at a table. I reminisce about how Ivor and myself met over three years ago. He blew the whistle on Vladimir Mashkov. He also stumbled on The Order that his dad was part of before he died. Then my thoughts go to Montenegro where we met up with him again to find out more about the organisation.

I stare at my engagement ring and wonder when this will be all over so we can get married.

JANE RETURNS in Tomorrow's World

Published by Thriller and Intense Limited

Copyright © 2021 by Leon Mark Anthony Edwards

This is a work of fiction. Names, characters, businesses, places, events, locales, and incidents are either the products of the author's imagination or used in a fictitious manner. Any resemblance to actual persons, living or dead, or actual is purely coincidental.

All rights reserved.

The moral right of the author has been asserted.

No part of this book may be reproduced in any form or by any electronic or mechanical means, including information storage and retrieval systems, without written permission from the author, except for the use of brief quotations in a book review.

www.leonmaedwards.com

❧ Created with Vellum

# PLEASE LEAVE A REVIEW!

Jane Knight A Spy Among Us

Thank you so much for buying and reading my book!!

This is my eighth book that I spent sixteen months writing. I have drawn from my own experiences to create my characters. They are not based on friends or family of real persons; apart from myself and fictional plot.

I mulled over the idea of writing my first novel in August 2016. I then found the courage to begin my first novel in December 2016. I did not finish my novel until March 2018. My wife and I became a family in June 2017. This postponed completing my first novel.

My first genuine review for this book was not until May 2020. I value my readers reviews because I then know they completed my book. Not half completed and never picked up again.

I plan on becoming a full time author by building up my catalogue of various genres that focus on Steamy, Hot & Passionate themes whether Romance, Action & Adventure or Thrillers.

# BOOKS ALSO BY LEON M A EDWARDS

Jane Knight Rogue Officer

Jane Knight Fair Game

Jane Knight Tomorrows World

Blind Love

Eternity Wing A Pray

To The Stars

Ponta Delgada A Good Place To Die

By Chance

# LEON M A EDWARDS CLUB

Join my Leon M A Edwards Club to receive future free ebook copies before release date.

I like to send out my books before I publish to hear from my readers.

Subscribe

The link above will take you to the subscription page.

Printed in Great Britain
by Amazon

64992352R00102